Paint the SUNSET

BOOK 3 – GOLDEN STATE TRILOGY
A CHRISTIAN CONTEMPORARY NOVEL

BY DAWN V. CAHILL

This is the land the sunset washes,
These are the banks of the Yellow Sea;
Where it rose, or whither it rushes,
These are the western mystery!

~Emily Dickinson

Cover design by Dineen Miller
Edited by Steve Mathisen, Odd Sock Proofreading
and Copyediting

To Albert, my biggest fan —and the mastermind behind the sardine prank. Thank you for believing in me, my love!

To Clyde and Dianne and the team, who faithfully obey Jesus by loving and feeding the poorest of the poor and sharing the gospel with them.

BOOKS BY DAWN V. CAHILL

Seattle Trilogy

When Lyric Met Limerick - Prequel
Sapphire Secrets - Book I
Moonstone Secrets - Book II
Emerald Secrets - Book III

Golden State Trilogy

Paint the Storm - Book I
Paint the Desert - Book II
Paint the Sunset - Book III

CHAPTER

Exultation is the going Of an Inland soul to sea— Past the houses, past the headlands, Into deep eternity!

~Emily Dickinson, SETTING SAIL

Meg closed her eyes and breathed in the warm Sunday spring breeze, background music serenading her. She couldn't think of a better song to accompany her and Jon on their boat, *Megatron*, than "Sailing" by Christopher Cross.

"Beautiful song, honey," she said to her husband, who stood in the cockpit gazing at the far-off silhouette of San Francisco, skyscrapers stacked atop dark hills. When he glanced back at her, she threw him a kiss, and he tossed her a wink. She grinned. They might as well still be honeymooning, even though they'd celebrated their second anniversary six months ago.

On Richardson Bay, the stresses of everyday life always dissolved into the sun-spangled water. Sailboats dotted the bay, their owners, drawn like themselves, to this perfect blend of cobalt sky and teal sea. The same good wind dancing and flirting with the *Megatron's* red-striped spinnaker lifted her ash-blonde hair as if it were a third sail. As the shoreline drew nearer, she reached for the binoculars, then saw Jon's son at the stern peering through them toward the Sausalito waterfront. She went to his side.

"Tanner, can you see your dad's shop from here?"

"Yeah. That homeless camp across the parking lot has doubled since last week." He shoved aside a lock of windblown dark hair. "There's a couple of old rusty RVs and even more tents than last time I saw it."

Her heart sank. The homeless camps kept multiplying all over the county, and apparently, nobody knew what to do about it. Or, more likely, competing agendas created an intolerable stalemate.

"Whoa," Tanner said, "what is he doing?" He adjusted the focus as if he couldn't believe his eyes.

"What? Who?"

He apparently didn't hear her. "No. Way."

"What, Tanner? Tell me what you're seeing."

"He's loitering by Dad's shop. See for yourself." Her stepson handed her the binoculars, and she directed them past the floating homes community, past the sailboat masts clustered like empty flagpoles at the marina, then zeroed in on Waterfront Industrial Park. She squinted. A figure did indeed appear to be snooping in the windows of *Paulson's Watercraft Service*. Right in broad daylight, not even attempting to hide. Brazen. She gasped. "I see him."

"He kind of …" Tanner's words died on the stiff, cool breeze.

She lowered the glasses, trying to interpret his expression. "He kind of what?"

Tanner shook his head and gazed over the water, frown lines cutting into his fifteen-year-old face. "Nothing. I'm probably wrong."

"Wrong about what?"

Another headshake. Meg couldn't decide if he was unsure or in denial about what he'd seen. "I can vouch that you really did see someone. We'd better alert your dad."

She rushed to her husband's side. "Jon, I think we need to get back and check that your shop is okay." She handed him the glasses. "Someone's hanging out there, looking in the windows."

A furrow popped on his forehead, and he lifted the binoculars, moving them right, then left, finally holding steady, adjusting the focus. "I don't see anyone. Are you sure?"

"Of course. Both Tanner and I saw someone."

He lowered the glasses and met her gaze, his brown eyes worried. "Well, they're not there now. But I'll motor back, just in case." He handed the glasses back, and she stood, feeling as helpless as a child while Jon spent the next few minutes maneuvering the tiller, steering the *Megatron* back to the shore. "We're only a couple hundred feet from the dock. I'll get us back as quick as I can."

At the yacht club, Jon and Tanner tied up the boat. In his haste, Tanner fumbled the rope and nearly dropped it into the water, pulling a swear word out of him. Jon, his brows folded together, ignored his son's colorful outburst. After what felt like ten minutes of muttering and agitated breathing but was probably closer to one or two, Jon finally stood and clasped Meg's hand. "C'mon, Tanner. To the car. Pronto." Meg, hurrying alongside him, hopped over the dock's uneven boards with care. Whoever they'd seen had plenty of time by now to get away. What would they find?

Tanner headed the opposite way from the car. "Dad, can I walk home?"

"Absolutely not. Son, in the car."

"It's only a mile." His feet didn't budge.

"I said no."

Tanner's pale face competed with Jon's stern expression. Meg wondered what the boy had seen to put that look there. She hadn't seen anything unusual other than the intruder. But Tanner must have, judging by his jerky yet reluctant movements. He slid into the car and down below window level, his long legs crammed against her seat. "Tanner, are you afraid someone will see you?"

"No."

"Did you see something that made you nervous?"

"I'm not nervous."

Meg couldn't decide if she believed him but opted not to pursue it. She gripped the armrest when Jon peeled onto Bridgeway and sped the quarter mile north to *Paulson's Watercraft Service*.

When they pulled into the parking lot moments later, multiple eyes from the trash-strewn camp followed them, and curious gazes stayed on them as Jon leaped out. Pulling her attention away from the onlookers, she watched Jon approach his shop door and look around. As she suspected, whoever had been there was nowhere to be seen. Jon checked the barred shop windows, peered inside, and backed away moments later scrutinizing the area behind him, to the left, then right.

"No sign of anyone," he said as he got in. "Even if they were scoping it out, that door is pretty solid, and there's a security camera outside. If anyone tries to break in, the alarm will go off."

As Jon put the Jeep in reverse, Meg caught movement—a hand, behind a tent flap, moved it aside, then a pair of round eyes peeped out of a narrow face hiding in the shadows. Next to the opening, a young man in black, probably late teens or early twenties, sat with his back to the tent, arms crossed. Sending smirks their way. Oozing attitude. Almost like he knew what they were looking for. He didn't resemble the intruder, yet he may have witnessed something. But his expression forbade any interrogations.

"Tomorrow, I'll look into a security upgrade for the shop."

Jon's words barely registered as she examined the man from the side so she wouldn't appear obvious. The burly scoper had worn a navy-blue shirt, but this young man was so slight he could easily pass for a tent pole. Why was he staring at them?

A fluffy cloud passed over the sun and sent an identical shadow of unease into her heart. Surely, the man staring at them had no hostile intent. Why would he? Because they drove a nice car? Because Jon was a well-dressed man? Homeless people were so unpredictable. Some were decent, others were up to no good. You just never knew.

Jon gripped the wheel and sped along the boulevard toward home. "Who would be stupid enough to try breaking through that solid metal door? I'm sure the shop will be fine. Whoever it was, they were probably just curious."

CHAPTER

Two

MYLA

Heaven is what I cannot reach! The apple on the tree,
Provided it do hopeless hang, That 'heaven' is, to me.
The color on the cruising cloud, The interdicted ground
Behind the hill, the house behind, - There Paradise is found!

~Emily Dickinson, *FORBIDDEN FRUIT*

"Shut up!"

Her eyes flew open, assessing her surroundings. Still inside the tattered, stinky sleeping bag, she squinted at the dawning daylight creeping through the tent flap. She inched open the flap to reveal a pile of trash on the cracked pavement. Crumpled snack packages, dirty rags, and the ever-present used needles. Awakened by someone's yells and the crunch of broken glass, she glanced along the row of makeshift tents—more like thrown-together tarp pieces set atop a concrete wasteland in Sausalito—she and twenty or so of society's throwaways currently called "home."

She dropped the flap. The angry words must have been hurled by the couple two tents over who constantly fought. She hoped they weren't yelling at their scrawny two-year-old. Maybe that's why he cried all the time.

She couldn't blame him. Many a time, she'd cried, too. Especially when thoughts of Lula—and Tyler—overwhelmed her. And constantly staring at Tyler's big white house on the hill didn't help.

Another shout, more garbled this time. Probably just Crazy Wesley, arguing with the imaginary voices in his head.

Desperate for another fix before the shakes hit, she squeezed her eyes shut as if she could force the sordid setting to vanish. Once the Oxy flooded her bloodstream, she wouldn't see the trash anymore—or hear the yells and cries. She wouldn't remember the part-time job she'd had last year, the shopping trips with friends. Nothing mattered anymore except getting high. And staying high.

Get high, stay high. Almost sounded like a sports team mantra.

Thrusting her hand under the air mattress, her fingers encountered something. The wad of cash. She collapsed in relief. Digging deeper, she touched the photo she'd had for a year, her most treasured possession.

Her sole memento of Lula. The baby girl waiting for her in heaven. And if she ever got out of here, she'd paint her baby's portrait and hang it where everyone would see.

A truck whizzing by shattered her melancholy musing. She forced herself to rise and pull a windbreaker over the sweats she slept in and then crept to the tent next door. JJ had asked when King-Boy would be making his rounds today. Plus, he might have a few extra pills to spare.

For a moment, she stood straight. Inhaling a deep breath of morning breeze, she allowed herself a momentary admiration of the Sausalito waterfront, where the rising sun cast golden sparkles across the vast, shining bay.

Nearby, someone cleared his throat. She didn't need to look to know who was watching her. She fingered the Swiss Army knife in her pocket. If he ever made a move on her, she'd poke his eyes out. He'd regret it the rest of his life.

Then she spun her gaze across the parking lot, and her whole body clenched as darkness filled her spirit. Her constant companion, Black Despair, refused to flee, even at the sight of a new day's glow.

Paulson's Watercraft Service announced the huge, black-beveled letters across the white stucco building.

If that jerk Jon Paulson hadn't fired her, she wouldn't be here.

She felt a small, satisfied grin curve her mouth. She wished she could see his face when he walked into his shop today.

Then another memory rose, choking her with bittersweet regret. Connor must never find out what she had done.

CHAPTER

Three

The homeless camp across the way had indeed doubled since last week. Jon Paulson, his heart heavy, pulled his Jeep into a parking space at his shop. If only he could single-handedly fix all their problems. But their problems were far too complex for one imperfect man to solve.

He got out and crossed the lot, conscious of the residents' eyes on him. What had happened to them to cause such destitution?

Sighing, he checked the knob on his shop's side door—locked. No signs of forced entry. Relieved, he swiped his key fob and stepped inside, inhaling the scent of old diesel and new chemicals. The daily noises of the industrial park—blaring ships, roaring truck cabs, laborers calling to each other—faded once he closed the door behind him. Dim daylight filtered through high, narrow windows.

Inside his dark shop, utter silence. At least until the day began in earnest at 9 a.m.

So far, he'd seen no sign of any unwelcome visitors. Priority number one for today: a new security system. He lifted the remote fob to disable the alarm, then made his way around crafts of all sizes on the 75,000-square-foot shop floor. Had he really been doing this for ten years? Seemed like just last year he'd taken over running the place after his father's unexpected death from a heart attack at age sixty.

His father would be proud of his upgrades and expansions. And all the creative ads he and the team came up with. Memories from his youth inhabited every square inch of the original section of the shop his dad had built. Memories of playing with toy boats and cars in the office as a young boy. Dad taught him, a young teen, the art of polishing aluminum and fiberglass exteriors to perfection. Eventually mastering Boat Engines 101. And later honing these skills as an adult into a five-star-rated shop and 89 percent favorable reviews on Yelp.

If not for the ever-increasing taxes and regulations California imposed on businesses, the place would make a decent profit. But this state had the unfortunate reputation of becoming one of the least tax-friendly in the nation. For weeks, an idea had percolated in the back of his mind. Should he relocate to a state with a more favorable business climate?

He hadn't brought it up with Meg yet, but he needed to soon.

Moving toward his office, he circled the rear of a sleek Fletcher Arrow motorboat and stopped, waiting for his vision to adjust to the dim light. Had that deep scratch on the boat's bow been there yesterday? He didn't recall noticing it or noting it on the work order. He continued toward his office to check the order, halting once again, and stared—his mouth agape. The wooden office door lay on the floor, busted as if someone had kicked it in.

He rushed for a closer inspection and curses he hadn't uttered for years flew from his mouth. File cabinet drawers hung open, papers were strewn across the floor, and the metal lockbox sat on his desk, yawning open. Hurrying to the cash box, he set it upright. Empty.

Yesterday, he'd counted at least five hundred bucks.

He scanned the desk and counters. The old laptop he hadn't used in a year should be in the corner. Missing.

He dug through the forced-open desk drawer, his fingers exploring its depths, seeking the cool surface of the monogrammed money clip Meg gave him on their wedding day. Worth over seven hundred bucks but priceless in sentimentality.

No money clip. Meg would be devastated, and not for the monetary loss.

Replacing the flimsy office door had dropped way down his priority list. He'd simply never imagined this would happen to him. He cursed again and did a visual check of the office window. The window was still locked, so he returned to the shop and inspected the rest of the doors and windows for signs of a break-in.

Nothing. How had the burglar gotten inside?

He went to the master light switch and flipped it on, then froze, unable to believe his eyes. If only this were simply a bad dream he'd wake from soon.

All ten boats sported some sort of graffiti or damage. Malcolm Johansen's red-and-teal Phleet Coventina motorboat had been vandalized on both sides with deep gashes as though someone had attacked the fiberglass exterior with an axe. Simplistic blue and black cartoons adorned Mr. Udell's Crestliner fishing boat and his daughter's Sundancer. He bent to study the images. Someone had drawn anime faces on the boat with magic markers. He'd seen those drawings somewhere recently. Shaking his head to dislodge the hidden memory, he peered over the edge of the Crestliner where the name *Pair O' Dice* struggled to be seen through spray paint.

Inside, more of the same. Streaks of spray paint marred the entire interior.

He hoisted himself up the ladder of Johansen's boat and nearly fell backward at the sight that greeted him. Someone had slashed all the bench cushions and also went crazy with the magic markers.

This couldn't be happening. He tried to shake away the vision, but the horrifying reality remained: tens of thousands of dollars in destruction, possibly hundreds of thousands. How on earth would he explain this to his clients?

Had Patti, his new assistant manager, locked up and set the alarm? His former assistant, Kevin Lipinski, would never forget to set the alarm. But Kevin had left California behind months ago for Portland and a new job with Phleet Powerboats as Production Manager.

He was being too hard on Patti. She must have set it because the alarm had beeped when he disabled it.

He swept his gaze around one more time. No sign of forced entry anywhere.

Had this been an inside job?

Nothing else seemed to be missing or out of place. The toolboxes sat undisturbed as though frozen in time. If only they had eyes and mouths, they could tell him who did this.

After calling 911, he got Patti on the phone and related what he'd found. His heart racing with shock, he glanced out the main door as if the perp might still be lurking. "Someone ransacked this place. You locked up, right?"

A sound on the other end could have been a muffled curse or a groan. "I most certainly did."

"Did you see anything or anyone when you left Saturday night?"

"Just that God-forsaken homeless camp across the lot."

Movement across the parking lot caught his eye. A couple of unkempt men paced outside the tents, smoking. "Did the custodians come by that night?"

"No, they're normally scheduled on Sunday evenings."

"I'll give him a call and ask if they saw anything."

"Want my take? I wouldn't be surprised if some of those blankety-blank homeless guys did it. You know how much they love graffiti."

"I didn't find any signs of anyone breaking in."

"You didn't? Now, that is odd."

"However, my wife and I both witnessed someone looking in the windows yesterday afternoon when we were out sailing. By the time we got back and checked it out, we didn't see anyone."

He described the intruder as best he could, and Patti's jaw sagged. "I bet he was from the homeless camp."

"If he was, he was hiding. Out of the few people loitering around the camp, I didn't see anyone who matched his description."

He ended the call and got the custodian on the line, who claimed not to have seen anything, or anyone hanging about, either. The man swore up and down he set the alarm and locked up. "Just like I do every time."

"Okay. I want you to know I appreciate all you do." Clicking off the call, Jon opened the warehouse's overhead door just as a cop car slid to a stop. Two men and a woman got out. The officers introduced themselves as Lee and Jackson and the woman as Ms. Wallace, the forensic lab technician.

The shorter cop, Lee, led the way. "Why don't you show us what you found."

It didn't take long for the two officers to agree they saw no visible sign of a break-in. Jon told them about the intruder, describing him to the best of his recall, and they inspected the damaged watercraft as Jackson snapped photos. Wallace dusted the office and alarm keypad for fingerprints. The guys on morning shift would start arriving any minute.

Lee stepped to his side. "Besides yourself, how many employees do you have?"

"Seven. My office manager, three full-time mechanics, and three part-timers."

"Will they all be here today?"

"No, one of my full-time guys is on vacation this week. And only two of the part-time guys are scheduled today."

"Okay. We'll need to fingerprint everyone at some point. How about vendors? Any who do business with you on a regular basis, such as custodians?"

"Yes, our custodians are a married couple, Tibetan immigrants. I just talked to him, and he swore he didn't see a thing."

"It would be helpful if we could get their fingerprints as well. Do you have security cameras here or nearby?"

"I don't have one inside." He'd never seen the need for such an invasion of privacy. He gave himself a mental kick for his laxness.

And now it was too late. "There's one outside in the parking lot that pans back and forth. I believe it's monitored by the warehouse next to mine." He pointed.

"We'll pay them a visit and review last night's footage. I hope you have good outdoor lighting."

"I do. There's a motion-activated light mounted above the side entrance and another one above the sliding door." Maybe the light and the camera captured last night's vandals.

Outside, he pointed at the dented cylinder over the doorframe housing the light. "Some loser smashed the dickens out of this, too." His spine prickled as the cops took photos. Apparently, the perp, or perps, had prepared for every detail.

He wandered back inside, the sense of unreality growing. Two employees joined them at the office door with stupefied expressions. Where would they even start with such a huge setback? Obviously, no one would get much work done this morning.

At Jon's request, Patti showed up early to answer questions, but her expletive-laced rant when she saw the damage shocked him. He'd never heard those words come out of her mouth.

She pointed to one of the magic marker images as the cops walked around taking photos. "Hey, Jon, recognize these drawings?"

"They look familiar. I was trying to think where I'd seen them."

"From Myla, that's who. Remember how she used to doodle anime images?"

"Ah, yes. But—what—what are you saying? You think Myla did this?"

"Who else? It's almost like she wanted us to know it was her. Stupid b—"

"She would've needed a key. Didn't she turn in her key fob?"

"She did. But maybe she kept a spare. I knew she was bad news."

Officer Lee interrupted her tirade. "Who's Myla?"

"Myla Delaney," Jon echoed. "A former employee."

A face popped into his mind. A cynical brunette with a chip-on-the-shoulder attitude. His former administrative assistant who'd shown keen interest in his expensive money clip.

Her empty, glazed-over eyes still haunted him.

Patti, her broad face etched in scorn, stepped next to Lee. "I don't think the person we're talking about axed the boats. She's not a large woman. But she loved manga, and she had mega-attitude."

Jon circled around for a better view of the axe marks. "Yes, someone physically strong made these gashes." Like the muscular intruder from yesterday?

Lee tilted his head at the destroyed craft beside them. "Those are pretty deep. Whoever did this used a lot of force."

Jon exhaled. "Maybe the guy we saw loitering was Axeman."

Too bad he or Meg hadn't gotten a better view of the guy. All they saw was long, dark hair, cutoff jeans, and a sleeveless blue tee covering a broad back.

"Patti, why would Myla do this?"

"Because she could," Patti snapped. "Remember how angry she was when we fired her? If you recall, she told us we'd be sorry. And look. She just brazenly waltzed in here and left her unmistakable mark."

Lee fingered his holster. "Can you get us the lady's address, please?"

"In a minute." Patti turned toward the office, then halted, pointing out the door. "Sir, do you plan to talk to those homeless lowlifes over there? Someone may have *seen* something."

Lee nodded. "Yes, we plan to interview them to see if anyone witnessed anything."

Jon lifted his head. "Patti, will you get Myla Delaney's address for Officer Lee, please?"

CHAPTER

Four

I measure every grief I meet With analytic eyes;
I wonder if it weighs like mine, Or has an easier size.
I wonder if they bore it long, Or did it just begin?
I could not tell the date of mine, It feels so old a pain.

– Emily Dickinson

Myla peeked out the flap of JJ's tent as two cops crossed the lot.

Straight at her.

She wrenched the flap closed. They couldn't be seeking her out. Nobody here knew her real name. Nobody from her previous life would ever recognize the plump brunette they remembered in her new emaciated, bleached-blonde persona.

Bowie, JJ's black lab, sat up, alerted by the cops' presence. She nudged JJ. "Hey, wake up. Cops are coming."

"Mom," he mumbled.

"No, not Mom, you idiot, it's Betty Boop."

He opened one eye. "Betty Boo-pah-doop. Betty Bop Bop…"

"Shut up." *Imbecile.* She punched his arm as male voices rumbled outside. "I said, cops are here."

"Wha' for?"

"Ssh." She rolled her eyes. JJ's brain cells were dissolving by the needleful. He should know very well why the cops had come.

Myla peeped through the flap. The cops were interviewing Mom. Like she knew anything.

"We think the break-in happened between ten p.m. and midnight," the shorter cop said. "Did you happen to see anyone lurking around the shop?"

"Me an' my old man, we dint see nothin'." Mom gestured across the lot. "We was sleeping like dogs till you come sniffing around."

"May I get your name?"

"Bernice Stoops, but ever'one round here calls me Mom. Me and Dad, my old man, we keep an eye on the place. He's like the camp bodyguard, y' know, and I make sure everyone has clothes and food." Pride brightened her deep voice.

If Mom only knew how well Dad kept an eye on *her*.

"And what is his full name?"

"Curtis O'Neal."

He's an ex-con, Myla wanted to shout. She didn't even want to know what crime he'd committed. Something vile, no doubt.

Another shout. The fighting couple were at it again. This time the child's wail overpowered the yells. It caught the attention of the taller cop, who headed to the tent. "Is everything all right?"

The couple quieted fast, but the toddler's cries continued. Myla would have to exit the tent in order to see what the cop was doing. She didn't dare show her face.

On second thought, why not? He would have no reason to connect her to Paulson's robbery.

Unless JJ opened his big mouth.

Inside the motionless sleeping bag, JJ snored away, so she crept outside on her knees. Would the cop take the child from his parents? God knew the poor thing deserved a far better home than this.

But the cop merely turned to his partner and said, "Notify DCFS to come out here and do a child welfare check."

Ha. The family would be gone before sunset. She returned to her own tent to make sure her little stash hadn't been stolen. *Note to self:*

don't leave your tent unattended. In her three months as a homeless throwaway, she'd had two bikes stolen, three packs of cigarettes, a sleeping bag, a camp stove, and a kerosene heater. Not to mention several packs of dollar bills.

She watched the cops return to the patrol car and drive away and then took out her phone, opened her Zinnia journal app, and started typing.

> Popo came by, but didn't know it was me they were looking for. Thank God.
> This place reeks, but JJ rocks. Don't know what I'd do without him.
> I miss Bhree. Should I text her? She probably thinks I'm dead. Wonder if Debbie and Reuben ever tried to look for me. They never got to meet Lula.
> Speaking of… I dreamed about her again last night. What else is new?

Five minutes later, JJ peeked into her tent, his eyes glazed over, spewing toxic waste about cops in general.

"Hey, they're gone," Myla reminded him. "They're never gonna find out who did it. Now, get in here and give me that Oxy you promised me."

The crying child from two tents over always made her think of Lula, who would never cry or speak. Or live. The pill slid down her throat. In moments, the drug swept away all memories like a rushing river of ecstasy coursing through her.

CHAPTER

Five

…Behind the dim unknown Standeth God within the shadow Keeping watch above His own.

~James Russell Lowell, THE PRESENT CRISIS

After the cops left, Jon called his wife. He simply needed to hear Meg's voice. She'd inject a measure of normality into this crazy morning.

"Hi, honey, you caught me at the perfect time." He could hear her half-panting the way she did when she was on a mission. "I'm just on my way to Linzee's to drop off a gift card for Ken's birthday. Can you believe they've already been married six months? And guess what? I got a text from Rich this morning. He and Kassidy are expecting a baby in September."

"Congratulations, Grandma." Talking about normal, everyday stuff like Meg's son Rich and her daughter Linzee helped keep his mind off the dreadful turn of events, if only for a few moments. "I knew you'd have grandkids before I did. Connor isn't even close to settling down, and Tanner, well, he's got a few years to go. Anyway, I called you for a reason. Ready for some bad news?"

Silence. He could have worded it better. Now she was on her guard. He recapped the morning's events, and Meg gave a groan of disbelief. "Most of the boats are completely ruined? Who would do such a thing? And why?"

"Patti thinks it might've been a former employee. I hope not, but sometimes dishonest people can fool everyone. For a while, anyway."

Since Meg had the day off work, she promised to bring him lunch and then said goodbye. He returned to the shambled office to find his insurance agent's number.

He glanced up when a shadow fell across the desk. "Jon," said Fred, his lead mechanic. He gestured toward a rear corner of the shop. "Come look."

Jon followed with reluctant steps. As if the morning couldn't get worse. Once he reached the dim corner, he saw the ugly black curse words beneath a blue manga figure marring the gleaming white coat of the Catalina. The yacht's owner planned to pick it up today. The spray paint had been applied to the most inconspicuous part of the boat, thus he hadn't noticed it earlier when the cops were here. While Fred scowled at the damage, Jon squeezed his head between his palms. "I don't know what I'm going to tell all these clients. They're going to be so irate and will probably never come back."

Hands shaking, he called the insurance agent, who promised to send someone out right away to evaluate the damage. After the assessor left, Jon spent an hour on a makeshift repair of the door. Not perfect, but it would hold until he could replace it. Spent and weary, he went to the sofa and cleared away the tossed papers, then plopped down, head in his hands. He hadn't even thought to pray. What kind of Christ-follower was he—to curse instead of to pray? His mood lightened when he remembered the small group fellowship he and Meg planned to attend tonight. They'd get the prayer and camaraderie he desperately needed.

"Mr. Paulson?" The two police officers stood in the open doorway. "We interviewed some of the residents of the homeless camp." Officer Lee stepped inside. "None of them claimed to witness the burglary. So, we're going to track down the former employee you indicated might be involved." He peered at his clipboard. "Myla Delaney."

"We'll let you know what we find." Jackson tapped his pen against the clipboard, and then they turned and left just as Jon's phone rang.

Carlos, one of the youth group boys from church, should be in school now. He couldn't have chosen a worse time to need Jon's help, but Jon couldn't let any of today's drama seep through.

"Carlos, my man. Are you at school?"

"I stayed home."

"Really? Are you sick?"

"No."

The silence on the other end throbbed with angst. Between him and Carlos, he was ODing on it. He needed to handle whatever this was with kid gloves. "Care to elaborate?"

Carlos' single mother must have left for her custodial job before her son got up. She would be upset he'd skipped school.

"I didn't have anything to wear."

Jon stared out the office window and focused his full attention on his young friend. "Oh, buddy, that's a bummer."

"My mom never did laundry this week." Probably because she worked two minimum wage jobs and didn't have time. "I borrowed a shirt from my older brother, but he ripped it off me."

If he recalled, fast-growing, thirteen-year-old Carlos had just three shirts which still fit him. "How about you help out your mom by getting the laundry caught up today?"

"We have no soap."

Jon's heart twisted. "Okay, how about I bring over some laundry soap tonight?"

The long pause thrummed. "Can you bring it earlier? I need clean shirts for tomorrow."

"I have a better idea. I'll call the church helpline and make sure someone brings you some new shirts and laundry soap today. Do you need anything else? You have enough food in the house?"

"We're out of bread and milk and meat."

"We're on it, buddy. Looking forward to seeing you play ball tomorrow night. Beat those Grizzlies, amigo."

Carlos chuckled. "Gracias."

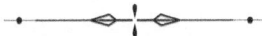

Linzee Tucker's face registered proper horror when Meg related the turn of events. Blonde hair swinging, sipping coffee in the San Rafael apartment she shared with her husband, she hadn't changed a bit since her wedding day six months ago. In fact, if it were possible to glow even more radiantly, Linzee did.

Until her coral-lipsticked mouth dropped, and her bronze-shadowed eyes widened at the tragic news. "Oh, no, Mom, I can't believe someone would trash Jon's shop. What are you guys going to do now?"

"I have no idea. I'm on my way over there now to see him."

Linzee chewed her lip. "So, it's not Ken's imagination. The crime around here really has exploded."

"If anyone would know, he would. What a dangerous world we live in now. You must worry about him."

Meg watched her daughter's knuckles turn as white as the cup her hands clung to. "Every day when he's out and about. I'm sure you've heard the stories about cop's marriages and how so many of them don't survive because of the stress of policing. And how many cops don't survive till retirement? I sure hope he doesn't become another statistic ..." She took a slow sip of coffee, her red boots tap-tapping on the stool leg.

Meg did the same while she gathered her thoughts. "This is probably the most delicious coffee I've had in a long time." A temporary digression until they returned to her daughter's morbid prediction.

"Thanks to Peet's Vanilla Cinnamon Coffee." Linzee pointed to a black box beside the Keurig. Meg breathed a prayer that her next words would not only go over well but be a source of encouragement to her troubled daughter.

"The two of you are probably the happiest newlyweds I've seen in a long time—"

"Did you hear about the shooting at that strip mall in Mill Valley? Ken was a block away when it happened." Linzee's boots kicked faster and harder on the stool leg as if it were responsible for the crime. "If he'd arrived one minute sooner, it might have been him on administrative leave instead of his colleague. Or worse, it could've been him that ended up dead."

"Oh, Linzee, I'm so sorry."

"This world sucks sometimes, doesn't it?" Her earlier joyous expression had morphed to a twisted mouth and downcast brows as if she were fighting back tears. "Makes me wonder if Ken and I should skip the baby-making. I'm not sure this world is a fit place to raise them anymore." She tossed back the rest of the coffee and bounded from her seat to put another pod in the Keurig.

Meg could think of no words to comfort her daughter right now. Linzee didn't want weak platitudes, and Meg didn't want to promote her own desire for grandchildren over Ken and Linzee's best interests.

Linzee thumbed hard on the brew button, taking out her angst on the innocent machine. "I don't see any signs things will get better."

Meg took another warm sip. "It's not like we haven't been warned."

"What do you mean?"

"I mean, Matthew Twenty-four. You know, when Jesus tells his disciples all about how horrible the days before His return will be."

"I'm going to have to read it again." Linzee leaned against the counter as she waited for her cup to fill.

Meg traced her finger along the veins in the faux-granite counter. "It's not a happy picture. And we shouldn't be surprised the world is in the shape it's in. But, if there's anything positive to be gained from it, we can be glad He's coming back soon to take us to our real home."

CHAPTER

The misfortunes of the disinherited of the world rouse in me not only compassion but a fierce indignation.

~Anne Sullivan

Meg parked her Mustang in the visitor lot at her husband's shop, dreading the moment of truth when she had to witness the destruction of her husband's livelihood. The shop contained his lifelong memories, his father's fulfilled dream. The culprits needed to be caught, and quickly, before they did this to someone else.

Wrinkling her nose at the odor wafting through the open driver's side window, she closed her eyes to block out the sight of a man relieving himself on the sidewalk.

Not something she wanted to see just before lunch.

God, help these poor people. I'm not even sure how to pray for them, but you know their every need, Lord.

God didn't reply, so she got out, then winced as her shoe landed on some broken glass with a loud crunch. She stepped back, barely missing a used hypodermic needle. Just feet away, several more lay scattered on a strip of bark dust. She slid back into the driver's seat, closed the windows, grasped the sack of homemade sandwiches, and then stepped onto the pavement again. This time she took extra care to avoid needles and glass.

"Excuse me, ma'am?"

A shabby woman stood a few feet from the warehouse next door. From her mismatched, baggy clothes, Meg concluded she resided at the homeless camp.

"My old man lost his job, and our grandkid hasn't eaten since yesterday. I was wonderin' if you had a couple dollars to spare."

Meg sighed but forced a smile. "Would your grandkid like a turkey sandwich?"

The woman's eyes shifted. "We was gonna go get 'im somethin' at the store. We just need a few dollars. Can you help us?"

Meg reached into the sack. "What's the child's name?"

"Um …" She mumbled something Meg didn't catch. "Whatcha got there?"

"A delicious turkey and swiss on rye." She held out a baggie-wrapped sandwich. "Here. Take this to your grandkid, and God bless you."

Judging by the lady's reluctant movements, she'd had her heart set on cold, hard cash. Meg wondered if she truly had a child living with her. Her long, matted hair draped over her hunched shoulders, and her hands shook with a slow, methodical rhythm. From drugs? Or some neurological condition? Meg's heart twisted. She longed to know the woman's story, how long she'd been homeless, and what had led to it. Had she once had a stable home and family life, then lost it all in a catastrophe? Or did her state result from a series of bad choices? Meg wondered if she'd had a traumatic childhood or spent part of her youth in foster care. She'd read that children who grew up in the foster system were far more likely to struggle with homelessness as adults.

If only she could delve deeper.

If only she could do more to help. "What's your name?"

"Mom."

"Mom?" She smiled at the woman. "That's my name, too. At least to my kids." Her attempt to connect fell flat. Mom merely stared at her. "How old is your grandchild?"

"Just turned eight." Mom tucked the sandwich into a large, flowered satchel. "Thank y' fer the food." She turned and shuffled off around the side of the neighboring building. Meg watched her enter one of the tents, wishing she had some gospel tracts to give the woman. The camp reminded her of photos she'd seen of third-world countries, where street living was commonplace. How could a rich nation like the US, not to mention the wealthy state of California, lack resources to solve this problem?

As Meg headed to Jon's office, the crew members nodded at her, lacking their usual friendly smiles. A distracted, heavy feeling permeated the atmosphere. Jon's face reflected it. She found him next to a beautiful cobalt-blue sailboat named Reina de la Mar. Queen of the Sea. Deep lacerations pockmarked its previously flawless surface. Unshed tears stung her eyes. God needed to rain down judgment on whoever did this.

"Hi, honey." She searched his face for any trace of his usual good humor.

Nothing. Just resignation, anger, and a flicker of something else behind it. Despair? But he lit up when he saw her.

"Hey." He took the sack she held out and then gave her a kiss. "Let me show you what they did."

She gaped at the damaged office. "Someone must have been really angry. Do you need help cleaning this up?"

"No but thank you. Mark, Fred, and I are on it."

"Is there security camera footage you can check?"

"There is. The cops are reviewing it." He retrieved the single sandwich from the bag. "Just one sandwich? Didn't you make one for yourself?"

She shrugged. "I gave it to a homeless woman. She claimed she had a hungry grandkid."

"I doubt she really wanted food."

"I agree, but I felt so bad for her." She waved away Jon's attempt to share his sandwich with her. "You eat it, honey. I can eat later."

"My wife and her heart of gold."

She lifted her hands in a what-else-could-I-do gesture. "Once my vacation's over next week, I won't have this kind of time to help. I might as well do it while I can." She joined him on the office sofa, one of the few items spared from damage. "I hope there are others who can help those poor people."

"I'm having mixed feelings about them. On the one hand, they're people Jesus died for, and I know he want us to help them. On the other hand, they're disrupting businesses all over the industrial park, not just mine. The cops do a sweep of the camp every few weeks, but the tents always eventually reappear, more numerous than before."

"I'm so sorry you're having to deal with this."

"My customer base has declined to the point where I was considering laying someone off. And now this." He swept his arm in an arc. "I might have just lost all my customers."

Meg caressed his shoulder blade as he slumped in defeat. "The city needs to find housing for those people."

"Speaking of which, the Business Chamber is meeting Wednesday evening to discuss that issue, and I plan to be there. Not sure anything will come of it, however."

The mess strewn around her feet felt like a slap in the face. "Did you find anything else stolen?"

The sudden twitch of his sandwich startled her.

"What?"

He chewed and swallowed, brows drawn, the very picture of a troubled man. "Actually, yeah. But you're not going to like it."

"Tell me." She held her breath, braced for bad news.

"The money clip you bought me is gone."

She sucked in a sharp breath. He might as well have punched her in the gut. "Oh, no. How terrible." Despite her sorrow, his appeared greater. Her arms circled his broad chest and pulled him to her. They sat side to side, heads touching, both equally victimized, helplessly comforting each other.

Jon broke the silence first. "Days like this make me want to pack up and get out of here."

Meg lifted her head. "I can't blame you for feeling that way."

"Seriously, I've been mulling over the idea for weeks now. Not only is it harder to run a profitable business anymore, but now the crime has gotten out of hand."

Thick pause in which she stayed silent. In his mood, she couldn't tell him how against the idea of relocating she was.

"Kevin and Alyssa Lipinski seem happy since they moved to Portland. At least according to their Facebook posts. They live in a suburb called Happy Valley, and he loves his job at Phleet Powerboats." He searched her face. "What do you think about relocating?"

She flinched. "You're truly considering this?"

"Only if you're on board with it too, love."

"Jon, I totally get why you want to move. But I have a new grandchild coming soon. This is my home. I love the beauty around here. The Golden Gate Bridge. My job. Moving away is the last thing on my mind. And what about your ministry with the youth at church? Who could possibly replace you for them?"

He nodded with a quiet sigh. "I understand." She could see the desperation etching grooves in his forehead. She hoped her resistance didn't make him feel squeezed into a corner with no escape in sight.

CHAPTER

Seven

To lose one's faith surpasses The loss of an estate, Because estates can be Replenished—faith cannot.

~Emily Dickinson, TO LOSE ONE'S FAITH—SURPASS

The longest, most frustrating day Jon could remember ended at five. He couldn't wait to leave. Most of the customers he'd spoken to today had either implied, or stated outright, he was to blame for lax security, and peppered him with questions. Could the damage be repaired, or would the insurance company have to replace the boats?

He had to tell them what they didn't want to hear. He'd determined just three boats could be salvaged with replacement parts, sanding, and new paint. But the rest were a total loss, and his insurance company would be buying those clients a new boat.

As he walked toward his Jeep, his fists tightened. He couldn't see the way to a happy ending here, which only fueled his eagerness to start anew somewhere else. With huge insurance premium increases, plus this blight on his formerly five-star enterprise, he didn't see how the business could survive.

Unlike his wife, he had no doubt the teen boys he mentored at church would be just fine. He couldn't be the only person with a heart for disadvantaged youth. Which reminded him—he needed to read the text Carlos sent him.

Hey Jon, thanks for the stuff. Someone brought me two shirts in size M and some food and soap.

No problemo, amigo. Call me anytime you need anything.

Now, back to business. His mind chewed on how to identify the vandals. The security guard at the warehouse next door told him the police had already confiscated the footage from last night. His curiosity would simply have to wait for them to get back to him.

At the homeless camp, a couple sat in chairs, their postures still and watchful. Instead of talking, they stared in Jon's direction. Uneasiness quickened his steps. He rounded the corner to the side lot where he'd parked his Cherokee, out of sight of the camp.

He rummaged through the glove box for his binoculars. Despite the cops' assurance, he couldn't shake his suspicion. He wanted to get a close-up of the couple watching him. Why, he wasn't sure. He found the perfect site beneath a weeping willow where he could zoom in without being seen.

The two turned to face each other, talking. Both young, one male, one female. Both were gaunt and wore sagging garments. The platinum-haired woman gave off a weary vibe, like an ancient soul disguising herself in a youthful body. The man, about the same age, had the defiant air of a longtime druggie.

The sad signs of ruin showed in their unkempt clothing and grooming. The woman had a familiar look, but Jon couldn't recall if he'd ever seen her, or she just reminded him of someone he'd known. She had probably been pretty—once upon a time. From here, her mouth appeared skewed to the side as though in a permanent sneer, and her short hair lay matted to her head.

All the way home, the couple haunted him. If his wife were here, she'd be praying by now.

With his gas gauge hovering at a quarter tank, he pulled into a Chevron station. As the tank filled, his cell phone rang. *Sausalito Police Dept.*

"Hello?"

"Mr. Paulson? Officer Lee. A couple of officers from Richmond PD went to Myla Delaney's address and talked to her mother. She hasn't seen Myla for several months and has no idea where she is."

"Okay." The nozzle clicked off, and he lifted it out. "Thanks anyway for having them check. What's your plan going forward for finding her?"

"We put out an alert. If she's found, we'll go talk to her."

His shoulders drooped at their lack of urgency. "Did you get a chance to review last night's camera footage?"

"We did. The camera must have panned away because it didn't pick up the custodian's arrival, but it did pick up their white van near the door. The only people the camera picked up were the apparent perps, two of them, a few minutes later. They crept along the side of the building, presumably to avoid the motion sensor, so we couldn't make out anything identifiable. Just two black shadows. One of them used an implement to bash the security light. Probably the axe they used to vandalize the boats. Then they opened the door and went right in. A third person joined them shortly after. Unfortunately, we couldn't discern their faces or physiques."

The sinking of his heart surprised him. Had he truly believed it would be so easy?

"Did you see the custodians leave?"

"Just the van, at ten thirty-one."

"Did anyone else exit? I'm curious how long the vandals stayed."

"Unfortunately, the camera didn't pick that up."

"Did you see if the people drove up in a car? Or what direction they approached from?"

"Didn't see a car besides the custodians'. If the culprits drove, they could've easily parked on the street and walked up. The camera pans the entire lot, but it missed their approach."

Jon tightened his already clenched jaw.

"You might want to invest in a good security camera," Lee advised.

Jon gave a skeptical headshake as he ended the call. Of course, he planned to upgrade his security. Assuming he stayed in business. In the meantime, they were no nearer to identifying the vandals.

His professional instincts, finely honed from years of trial and error, were trying to tell him something.

Lee and Jackson needed to try a little harder to locate Myla Delaney. Because if they wouldn't, he would.

To: SausalitoJon
From: KevinLipinski

Hey, Jon, thanks for the email. Good to hear from you. Sorry to hear of your recent misfortune. Yes, we're very happy here in Portland. How can you not be when you live in a suburb called Happy Valley? LOL. We live on a wooded hillside with an amazing view of Mt. Hood. The job is going well. I can definitely keep my eyes and ears open for a sales or management position at Phleet that you might qualify for. We're always hiring. Even though the business has been around for only ten years, it's exploding! We're already the nation's number one in sales volume in the industry. Will keep you posted!

After a quick internet search, Jon learned Phleet Powerboats, Inc., had successfully branded itself by naming all its boats after Greek and Roman sea goddesses. Its founder, Portland native Liz Williamson, a graduate of Oregon State's engineering program, had earned a fortune by designing powerful, aerodynamic speedboats with unique color combinations and marketed them to wealthy young millennials. Ms. Williamson, daughter of a speedboat racer, had apparently done something right. Last year, Phleet cracked the Top 10 in revenue for all Oregon companies. Jon visualized his client Mr. Johansen's damaged red-and-teal Coventina. To his middle-aged eyes, it had always appeared a bit gaudy. Obviously, he wasn't Phleet's target market. But it wouldn't stop him from giving it his all if he were to work for them.

> Sorry your wife is not enthusiastic about moving, but maybe, in time, she'll come around. Tell her that Alyssa is really enjoying the new neighborhood and church. Social opportunities abound!

> Kind regards,
> Kevin

CHAPTER

Eight

The tick of the faux-wood wall clock made an ominous echo in the quiet of Meg's she-shed. With a pang of bittersweet nostalgia, she relived the romantic day at Fisherman's Wharf when Jon bought it for her, then returned her attention to the mess of color and shapes on the canvas in front of her.

Taking out all her angst on brushes and canvases usually calmed her distress. But not today. "God," she moaned, sweeping size 10 and 12 brushes across the paper. "What is to happen to Jon and me?"

Most days, the sun struggling through the dusty windows of Jon's backyard shed, which she'd turned into her paint studio, made her miss her sun-filled, fully furnished studio at her San Rafael home. Today, she'd learned Rich and Kassidy had repurposed it as a newborn nursery—a far more important use than a mere hobby.

The evening sun sent a soft apricot glow into the shed as she flicked on the easel's overhead lamp. She picked up a round size 6 and covered the middle with Mauve Blue, then blended in some Winsor Red and Orange. "His dream has died, God ... crumbled to ashes ..." Time for Silver and Pewter. More dabbing, more tense streaks. A heap of boulders took shape before her, and she stepped back. A jagged wall, newly collapsed, loomed behind the rocks. She dipped a size 2 brush into Ultramarine Violet and dabbed two silhouettes standing atop the wall, looking down on the ruins. A subconscious rendering of her and Jon's life? She and Jon stood superimposed over an orange glow hinting at a setting sun ... the end of his father's legacy?

Tears streamed down Meg's cheeks. She found a clean spot on the paint-spattered rag beside her and wiped away the wetness. "And now Jon wants to leave it all behind. How can he ask me to leave my life here?" Even though their quality of life may have declined, it was as familiar to her as her scruffy old red slippers.

She didn't want a new pair of slippers.

She wanted her comfortable old slippers of a life back.

"Why did you do it, Myla?" Through a cloud of smoke, Jon Paulson and his son Connor reached long, thin arms at her, their fingers transforming to claws. Scrambling backward, she strove to evade their sharp weapons. Connor's reproachful gaze bore holes in her.

Her former friend must hate her. "It wasn't my idea!" she shouted back. "King-Boy talked me into it!"

It was like they didn't even hear her. "Fire!" Connor shouted, sneering as he shook his fist at her. She'd never seen this side of him, didn't know he was capable of such animosity.

Jon's visage grew larger, nearer. "Someone call 911!" The voice that emerged from him came out high, hysterical, like a woman's. "Help us!"

Connor hovered above her, a disembodied face like the Cheshire cat. "You better get out now!" A siren blared, and she turned to run, but the smoke blinded her, and she slammed into something. A brick wall materialized under her frantic fingers as the siren grew louder, along with Jon and Connor's shouts.

She opened her eyes, and grim reality intruded. No Jon Paulson, no Connor loomed over her. Merely a grimy tent doing a poor job of blocking out the yelling outside. And the siren still blared, even nearer. Was someone in trouble? Infused with sudden energy, she bolted upright, breathing deeply.

Smoke!

JJ still snored beside her, and she lifted the tent flap. An ambulance stood fifty feet away, whirling lights coloring the dark night. Paramedics shouted as they rolled a stretcher toward a haggard RV and tried to shoo away the growing crowd.

Smoke billowed from the vehicle's underside, interrupting the night with its angry plumes. Someone's propane tank likely caught fire. She should be used to these weekly-or-so ambulance visits by now, but shock still accompanied its unwelcome visit.

She hadn't met the RV family but recognized the pacing couple holding hands. She knew they had two school-aged girls, so where were they? If she were the praying type, she'd be casting petitions to a Higher Power to make sure those poor kids were alright.

A fire truck careened alongside the ambulance, wasting no time spraying the inferno. Two firemen rushed into the RV, then reappeared moments later, each carrying a child. Myla rushed over, but the paramedics yelled and gestured for her to stay back.

"Are they alive?" she shouted. They nodded and proceeded to load up the ambulance. Once it drove away and the firemen extinguished the danger, she made her way back to her tent and dove inside.

No way would she sleep now. Her life had become a melting pot of guilt, fear, and desperation. The homeless condition cheapened life. Injury and death were so commonplace here—nobody batted an eye anymore.

She cringed, imagining what her old friends would think if they could see her now. Especially Connor, as decent a person as they come.

Whatever her future held, there was no place for anything good.

CHAPTER

Nine

Richard St. John awoke with the sun beaming in his eyes. Light jabbed into his throbbing head as if it had switched on the headache.

Would this daily morning misery never end?

"Good Lord. Kassidy?"

The sound of running water from the master bathroom told him his wife was in the shower. A little warm water therapy might alleviate the headache.

He eased out of bed by sliding to the floor feet first, then carefully rolling his body upward. As he stood, he anchored himself on the headboard until his head stopped spinning. Now, time for a shower. But first, he snagged his prescription bottle of OxyContin and swallowed two. He checked the remaining pills, then the refill date. Crap. He would run out before the pharmacy would allow a refill.

He'd worry about it after Kassidy left for work. Stepping into the bathroom, he inhaled steamy air, which eased the throbbing a millimeter. "Can I join you, hot stuff?" He stripped and stepped into the watery enclosure.

"Of course, Mr. Hotness. What are your plans for today?"

After he planted a kiss on her lips, he gazed into her gorgeous gray eyes. "I *plan* to keep looking for a job. Good thing my mom got you that job at Noelle Marquette, or we'd really be hurting."

"I know, right? I love going into the city every day, working for one of the most prestigious department stores in the country. Surrounded by luxury apparel."

"And you fit right in, my luxurious wifey." He ran a scented bar of soap along Kassidy's slightly rounded middle. "You won't be able to stay on your feet in a few months. Then what will you do?"

"I don't know. Find a desk job? Hopefully, by the time the baby's born, you'll have a steady job. What about Jon's shop?"

He squirted shampoo on his hands and worked it through his wet hair. "I'd love to work for Jon and tinker with boats all day. But the tremor in my hands limits my job possibilities."

"But the doctor said it would go away with time. It's already been a little over a year since the shooting."

He cringed at the word as he rinsed his hair. Even though he had nearly recovered from the head injury that left him in a coma for three weeks, the residual effects still plagued him. Headaches. Trembling hands.

"Did you ever ask your dad about getting on at Intel?"

Warmth began to creep along his limbs, and a glow nestled in his chest as he towel-dried his hair. The Oxy at work. "Nah, that's too far of a commute. I'd rather not have to drive sixty miles on the 880 twice a day. What kind of a life is that?"

"But it's great pay, Rich. And eventually, we'll want to move out of this house and get our own place, right?"

Finally feeling as pain-free as he ever got, he buried his face in her wet, scented hair. "Mmm hmm. But I'm not in any hurry to move out of here as long as Mom keeps giving us such a great deal on rent."

Kassidy fell silent, and Rich knew it was only temporary. Tonight, she'd bring it up again. Maybe by then, he'd be feeling so good, he'd tell her what she wanted to hear.

The water fell on them in equal measure, yet between the two of them, the gulf yawned ever wider.

Once Kassidy had left for her long drive into the city, Rich wasted no time opening a browser on his phone. He keyed in the website he knew by heart but hadn't saved to his favorites, just in case his wife or anyone else happened upon it. He ordered a two-week supply of Oxy with the credit card Kassidy didn't know about and added extra for rapid shipping so it would arrive in two days.

There. Now he didn't need to worry about running out of painkillers. He was set.

CHAPTER

Ten

Meg parked next to the weeping willow in the shop's parking lot, a rare spot of green in this expanse of concrete and hard edges. She squinted against the noonday sun reflecting off the corrugated-metal shop roof. "Ready for this, Bestie?"

Camille Patterson hoisted the sack of sandwiches to her lap and leaned around Meg to get a better look at their destination. "Completely. Let's do this." She chuckled. "I bet this wasn't how you envisioned spending your staycation, was it?" Then Camille's smile disappeared, and Meg swiveled to see what wiped the joy from her ever-cheerful friend. The tarp-covered bundles scattered around the camp must have replicated overnight, along with a couple of battered minivans stuffed with trash, parked near the tents.

"People actually live in those cars?" Camille's horrified whisper sizzled with disbelief. "With their kids?"

"I know, it's terrible." Meg got out. "Careful where you step."

"So you said. At least twice."

Meg texted Jon that she'd arrive soon, and they approached the tent city. Camille cradled the sack of sandwiches to her chest as though reluctant to part with them. More likely, a defense mechanism from not knowing what they might encounter. Last night, between the two of them, they'd slapped together ten sandwiches.

A middle-aged couple loitered outside one of the vans. The skin on their jowls sagged, and double chins wobbled as they turned their heads to stare. Meg plastered on a friendly smile. "Hello there. We have some PBJ sandwiches here."

Camille held up the sack. "And some apples and bananas."

"Would you like some food?"

The man grinned wide, revealing misshapen, discolored teeth. At least the few remaining teeth. "Couple o' do-gooders, yeah?" He gave a raspy chuckle. "Scorin' points with the man upstairs?"

"No, we ..."

"Lookie here, Mama. Lunch."

His raised voice gathered a small crowd, and soon Meg and Camille had passed out several sandwiches and some gospel tracts. Meg was astonished at the variety of people who called this place home. A couple of older gentlemen, all bushy whiskers and eyebrows, sat on yellow crates. One rocked back and forth, a nonstop human pendulum, muttering nonsense. A young couple with angry furrows and contemptuous sneers tugged the hand of a teary-eyed little blond boy. Dressed in a spotless sailor suit, he could belong in one of the palatial stucco homes on the wooded hillside overlooking this sorry place.

Cute little tyke. His shoddy parents made sure he dressed nicely, even at the expense of their own appearance. Meg gave each of the three a sandwich.

A shout echoed behind her, and she jumped. Turning her head, she noticed the rocking gentleman had stood and was shouting obscenities at something only he could see. Another man near Meg chuckled. "Don't be scared. That's just Crazy Wesley. He sounds dangerous, but he's super harmless."

She forced a smile at the unkempt man in a soiled jumpsuit and made haste away from Crazy Wesley. A young woman stood off to the side, watching the proceedings with a smirk, her skinny arms crossed over her black tee shirt like a shield. Meg guessed her age as late teens, despite the tough demeanor. Crisscrossing the sidewalk, Meg held out a sandwich. "Would you like a freshly made peanut butter and jelly sandwich?"

Eyeing the baggie suspiciously, she took it and turned it over and over as if it might be a trick. "Thanks," she muttered in a voice like aged leather, a voice hardened, Meg gathered, from years of delinquent living.

Camille materialized beside her. "What's your name?"

The girl scratched at her leopard-skin leggings. "BB."

"Hi, BB. I'm Camille, and this is Meg."

The girl, still scrutinizing the sandwich, uttered something that sounded like "meh."

Meg smiled. The girl reminded her a little of her daughter, Linzee, during her rebellious phase. "Is BB short for something?" She kept her tone casual so as not to stir up the girl's defenses.

"Betty Boop."

A chuckle began in Meg's throat before she caught herself. "Really." A 1930s cartoon character was the last thing Meg expected. "Was your mom a Betty Boop fan?"

"My grandma." BB still hadn't met Meg's eyes. Her gaze wandered everywhere except to her and Camille. "She said I had a face like Betty Boop's. Always called me BB."

The young woman's elfin features and wide brown eyes contrasted with her toughened voice and body language. Meg, surprised and pleased to have gotten this far, wasn't about to probe further for BB's actual name.

BB turned and hollered behind her. "Hey, JJ. Get your butt out here."

A loud grunt, followed by movement in the tent, then a sunken-cheeked man around BB's age emerged, a black lab at his heels. Meg stifled a gasp as she recognized the guy who'd watched them the day before the break-in. Had he been involved?

41

The young man rubbed his eyes. "Yeah?"

"These ladies brought sandwiches." She handed him hers. "Here. Eat."

JJ, a skeletal young man in shorts and a tank top, looked at the sandwich like it was poison. "Not hungry." Tattoos covered his arms and upper chest but couldn't hide the ugly needle marks crisscrossing his skin.

Had heroin or meth turned him into a walking, talking skeleton? Meg thought she detected a spark of something like intelligence flashing through the haze in his eyes. Maybe he was one of those tragedies she'd read about where gifted young men and women get derailed by addiction. One bad choice, one unscrupulous friend, and even the brightest of kids could end up here.

She wished she had some dog food for the lab. His ribs protruded through his dull coat. How many meals a day did he get? The dog, watching her, responded to her attention with a hesitant wag.

JJ swayed, opened his mouth, and a familiar tune emerged. "I fight reality, reality always wins ..." Although the words slurred, he sang in an unexpectedly melodic voice.

Meg recognized the melody from the '80s. *Authority Song*, different lyrics. "You have a nice voice."

Either he didn't hear her through his drug-induced stupor, or he ignored her. "I fight reality ..."

BB rolled her eyes. "He's so John Legend. Always singing."

Camille raised her brows like an America's Got Talent judge. "He's really good." Her voice trailed off, and Meg filled in the blanks. *What is a talented singer like him doing in a place like this?* All the more tragic to realize what he could have been.

Just as abruptly as he began singing, he turned and disappeared into the tarp-covered shelter he'd come from. The tarp's edge didn't reach the ground. Inside the gap, she could see a bicycle, crates and boxes, and the edge of a stained mattress. Messy piles of rags. Or possibly clothes. Outside the gap was strewn a mix of food cartons and scraps. Rat magnets. Meg shuddered at the thought of any human living in such an environment.

It could almost make a person feel guilty for living in a normal home with fresh food, running water, and utilities.

These precious people, made in God's image, lived like animals. Her spirit, weighed down in sorrow, could only lift a silent, helpless prayer to the heavens.

CHAPTER

Eleven

I'm nobody! Who are you? Are you nobody too? Then there's a pair of us—don't tell! They'd banish us, you know.

~ Emily Dickinson

Myla scratched Bowie behind his ears, and the dog gave an appreciative woof. JJ'd been here two weeks, and BB still didn't know his story. "Were you in a band or somethin', brah?"

From her sleeping bag, JJ's slitted gaze regarded her. "Nah. Going to be someday, dude."

Cross-legged next to him, she shifted so the hard ground wouldn't dig into her bones. "Did you graduate?"

"Yeah. I was a salute—salutator … you know what I mean."

She raised her eyebrows and sighed. "You were one of 'them.'"

"One of who?"

"Those dudes. The ones everything came easy for. I bet you went to college. Didn't you?"

"Yeah." His voice was losing steam, and she nudged his leg. "Went to Cal State my freshman year."

She wrinkled her nose against the pungent BO-and-weed odor emanating from him. Despite his ripeness, she needed him. He was her only true friend. As a bonus, whenever Bowie was by her side, Dad left her alone. He and everyone thought Bowie was much fiercer than he really was. "What's JJ stand for, anyway?"

"Justin James Cooper. In high school, they called me Just or James the Just."

"Sounds royal."

He chuckled.

"So why are you here? How'd you get hooked on Oxy?" She nudged his arm this time. "I want all the deets."

"I got injured at work and got a prescription for pain meds. They helped, but I couldn't work. Couldn't concentrate on classes. Life sucked, man. Then my stepdad kicked me out, and I went to live with an aunt. Eventually, her boyfriend kicked me out. A friend of mine offered to share his tent with me. And I ended up here."

"Where is he now?"

"He bit it."

In her former life, a mention of death would have shocked her. Now ... nothing.

"Did you have Bowie then?"

The dog, hearing his name, thumped his tail against a tattered armchair with its stuffing falling out.

"I found him before I moved here. Someone had left him behind. I walked up to him, and he just looked at me with them eyes like he was saying, 'Will you be my human?'"

"Ah, poor doggy."

JJ's head flopped to the side, and he patted the space beside him. "C'mere, keep me company."

She obliged, and they lay on their backs together, hand in hand, staring at the tarp rising to a peak above them. "Sometimes, I wonder what it's like to die." The thought didn't frighten her. The friends she'd known who OD'd looked so peaceful in death—their faces untroubled, their eyes blinded to the horrors of life.

"Me too."

She turned her head and studied his profile. Strong bone structure. Straight, shoulder-length brown hair, smooth and combed. His pride and joy, he called it. Surprising, considering JJ only managed to shower and shampoo whenever Dad could get his car working and drive them to the Y.

If King-Boy weren't in her life, she might want more from JJ than mere friendship.

JJ caught her looking and pulled her hand to his chest. "If I ever die, I promise I'll come back and tell you what the other side is like." He broke into a hum, and she recognized the tune as an old '60s song. The Doors. *Break On Through (To the Other Side)*.

"I love it when you go all Jim Morrison on me," she told him, snuggling against his side.

He squeezed her hand. "Your turn. Tell me all your deets."

"All my deets." Her voice dropped as her mind wandered back to last year. "I can offer you sad deets or happy deets. Which do you wanna hear first?"

Her newborn baby girl appeared at peace. And oh, so cute. Everything on her was miniature—knuckles, earlobes, toenails like teeny-tiny shell fragments. Lula's soft head could fit inside Myla's palm.

They'd allowed her a few minutes to hold her baby before they took her away. They said she was dead. Lula couldn't be dead. The doctor must have lied. Myla unwrapped the blanket to check Lula's breathing for herself and laid her palm on the baby's belly.

Nothing!

She placed her finger on Lula's nostrils. Still nothing.

Her heart jackrabbited in her chest. She fought for breath, and a scream pierced the air. Then she realized it was her own.

Two nurses came running. One tried to wrest Lula from her arms.

She squeezed her daughter to her chest. "No! You can't have her! She's mine." Her whole body heaved. The pain from her cesarean incision felt like a fiery knife across her belly.

"Shh, dear, I know it's hard." The nurses' platitudes went on and on, and finally, when Myla's sobs had weakened her grip, they took her baby away.

The doctor prescribed OxyContin for her incision pain. It totally worked. As a bonus, it also took away the constant ache of baby loss. At least temporarily.

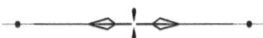

"I didn't know you had a baby." JJ shifted to embrace her.

"She'd be a year old."

"Who's the dad? King-Boy?"

She nudged his leg with her toe. "Huh uh, King-Boy was later on."

"I bet you know King-Boy's real name."

"I do, but I can't tell. He'd kill me. Anyway, he ain't my baby daddy. That was DJ. King-Boy's stepdad. Remember?"

"Oh, right. That dude."

"You can see DJ's house from here," Myla said. "The white one on the hill over yonder." She pointed in the direction of the wooded hillside to the west, even though JJ couldn't see it from inside the tent.

"Which white one? There's, like, five o' them on that hill."

"The big one on the very top."

"Really? Wow. I know the one you mean." The awed edge to his voice didn't come around often. "How come he's so rich?"

She rubbed her fingers together. "Drug money."

"I want me some o' that drug money." He heaved a sigh. "How'd you meet such a rich dude?"

"I was living with my foster parents, Debbie and Reuben. DJ was Debbie's brother. He turned out to be a two-timin' son-of-a—"

"Was he a deejay?"

She scoffed. "Of course, he wasn't a deejay. That's just what I called him. Short for Despicable Jerk. His name was Tyler."

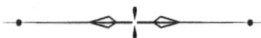

The family had gone camping to celebrate her seventeenth birthday at Lake Tahoe … Debbie and Reuben, Myla, and, at the last minute, "Uncle" Tyler and his two sons.

It was 14-year-old Tyler Jr, called Tye, who'd turned her on to pot for the first time. And later, Green Goblins. He was the one who showed her how to break open the little green pill and extract the tiny capsule of pure morphine inside. "I can't believe your dad lets you do this," she told him.

"Are you crazy? You think I'd tell him?"

"Don't you get them from him?"

"Yeah, but he doesn't know. I just help myself when I get the chance." He explained how he went about obtaining the pills without his dad's knowledge, and Myla marveled at his deviousness. You'd never know from the soft planes of his smooth face he was well on his way to hardcore drug addiction.

She remembered her first opioid high with Tye underneath the weeping willow on the corner. She thought she'd died and gone to heaven. The euphoria was so otherworldly. Something happened to her that day. Something strong and dark swept over her, something courageous and fierce. It began eroding the gentle, people-pleasing Myla her friends knew, the Myla with uncertain boundaries—and replaced her with an older, cynical soul with hard edges and a screw-you attitude.

She became Iron Woman. Nobody would ever take advantage of her again.

Eventually, Tye introduced her to his stepbrother, who insisted she call him by his street name, King-Boy. He'd reminded her a little of Justin Bieber and she almost laughed when he showed her the dark, monstrous tattoos wrapped around his bulging biceps. But the tough, un-Justin-Bieber-like glare he bulleted her way stopped her laughter just in time.

At first, she felt no attraction. She was still crushing on King-Boy's stepdad. She remembered when it all began, the cool, sunny day at the lake with the divinely handsome "Uncle" Tyler, who'd shown up without his CPA wife. "She had a deadline she couldn't get out of, told us to go on without her." His meaningful look at Myla communicated volumes.

Later the same night, when he poked his head in her tent, she invited him in. She'd purposely pitched her tent far away from the others just in case her fantasies came true. "And I thought you were such a nice, sweet girl," he chuckled.

No more Miss Nice Girl.

Tyler paid for expensive vacations for the whole entourage—Debbie, Reuben, and Myla, along with himself, his wife, his two sons, and two stepsons. She and Tyler always stayed careful not to let the attraction between them leak out in front of his family. By design, they stayed as far away from each other as they could. She spent time with his sons and stepsons, getting to know them, but once they got back home, she and Tyler rendezvoused in his office or in luxurious hotel suites. He, along with Tye's drug supply, brought her out of the cursed prison she'd built around herself like bricks of artificial sweetener.

After the night at the lake, she thought she'd never tire of him.

Until she found out she was pregnant.

JJ's eyes lit with curiosity, probably from the most exciting story he'd heard in this place of loss and suffering. "Did your foster mom know her brother was your baby daddy?"

"Well, I didn't exactly tell her who the daddy was. I told her it was a one-night stand, and I planned to keep the baby. Her brother was an upstanding member of the community, and I figured she wouldn't believe he'd gotten me pregnant. Then she told me she couldn't support a baby along with me, so I decided it was time to track down my bio mom. She has a lot to answer for."

"What happened to the son?"

"Tye? Now that's a sad story. He dropped out of high school, and last I heard, he was living on the streets of Vegas."

"When did you start working for the dude over there?" He pointed in the general direction of *Paulson's Watercraft Service.*

"Started when I was a few months pregnant. Before I started to show, so they wouldn't use it as an excuse not to hire me." She whispered into his shoulder in case anyone was hanging around outside. Nobody but JJ knew her history with the shop or needed to know. "I took some time off after having Lula and went back. Same thing that happened to you happened to me. The new office manager was a real b.... She told me I had to get a drug test. I tried to refuse, but then Jon, the owner, got involved and told me either I get the test or get fired. So, I did the test. The Oxy showed up, and he fired me."

"Sucks."

"Yeah. Big-time. Since then, I haven't driven a car, painted, or played my bongo drum."

"You're a painter? Like, with actual oil paints?"

"Yep. Acrylics, oils, markers, everything." She picked up an empty spray paint can in the corner and rattled it at him. "And this."

"And you play the bongo too."

"Used to. But someone stole it." She balled her fist, wishing she could punch the culprit. Her bongo could've earned some decent sidewalk dough.

"Someone stole my guitar, too, and all the dough from my gig."

"Is that why you don't sing on the corner anymore?"

He nodded. "Bowie just sat there and barked at them. But it didn't stop them." He traced her cheek with a soft caress. "How'd you end up here?"

She decided to tell him a mere fraction of the truth. No need for him to know the whole story, especially one that made her cringe whenever she thought about it. "My mom harassed me all the time, constantly on my case about one thing or another. I had to leave, but I had no other place to go. Like you."

"No place to go." He heaved onto his side, brimming with sudden alertness. "Like the saying goes. 'There is nothing to learn, nothing to attain, nothing to explain, nothing to do, and no place to go.'"

She gripped JJ's hand harder. "Yep. That's us."

CHAPTER

Twelve

... From the patient and the low I will take the joys they know; They shall hunger after vanities and still an-hungered go.

~ William Vaughn Moody

Over at Ooh Lah Latte, the local coffee shop, Myla and JJ found a table in the corner, far from the judgmental patrons eyeing them with disdain or pity or revulsion—or all of the above. Yet Myla could pretend she was one of the normal people when she plugged in her smartphone (thank you, US Government) and ordered a mocha, like anyone else (thank you for the cash, Jon Paulson). Or when she used the bathroom and scrubbed away at the foul odors hovering over her 24/7 now (thank you, Corporate America).

King-Boy didn't seem to mind her "Eau de Campground" scent when she met him behind the warehouse last night. Still, she wished she'd had a chance to clean up before their tryst.

She returned to the table with two coffees in hand. JJ had found a Marin Mercury and was scanning it with his glazed eyes. Myla doubted he was reading it. She waggled her finger at him. "Hey, let's check out the police log." She scooted next to him and wrested the paper out of his limp grasp. She lowered her voice. "I wanna see if you and I and King-Boy made the news, if you know what I mean."

JJ chuckled. "Yeah. That was so much fun."

"Whatya mean, fun?" she muttered. "You just stood there being all cheerleader. He and I did all the work." She ran her fingertip down the page until she found what she sought. "Ha." She lowered her voice to just above a whisper. "Here it is. 'Monday, 8:25 a.m. Police were called to *Paulson's Watercraft Service* after the owner found the shop vandalized and some cash stolen. Police are seeking a former employee who may have some information on this case. Please call Sausalito Police Department if you have any leads.'"

She cursed. "A former employee, huh? Do they mean me?"

JJ stared at her, a spark of interest piercing his hazy eyes. "You're busted, girlfriend."

She scoffed. "They ain't gonna find me. I'm like *The Purloined Letter*. Right under their noses, where they least expect me to be. Ha."

"I read that story my freshman year. Honors English." JJ removed the coffee cup lid and poured in a stream of sugar, then another, with shaky hands. "How does your old boss know it's you?"

She took a sip of pure black coffee. "Probably that witch, the office manager, recognized my drawings. I bet she still hates me."

"In that case, we need to be moving along. I'm not going down if you do. This was all your idea."

"It was not." She tossed him a dirty look. "You better shut up, big mouth." A shadow fell across their table. Dad, his arms folded, leered at them.

"Dad." She kept her voice carefully neutral.

Dad pointed at JJ. "Mom needs you for something."

Myla's heart lurched, and she sent a frantic headshake toward JJ, who apparently missed her distress, missed the obvious clue that Dad wanted to catch her alone.

"Let him stay," she snapped at Dad. "Mom can get someone else."

But JJ was already on his feet, lurching toward the door. She rose to join him.

"You." Dad pointed at her. "Stay. It's important."

I'm not a pet dog, you jerk.

Still on her feet, she glared at him. "If you want to talk to me, I'll be in JJ's tent."

"I know what the two of you did the other night. What if I were to let the cops know?"

He had to be bluffing.

"You don't know nuthin."

"If you keep acting all snooty and stuck-up to me, I'll tell the cops." His sneer poked a hole in her defenses. She focused on a spot above his head.

In other words, if she didn't let him have his way with her, she was screwed.

Either way.

She couldn't let him see her fear. She flared her nostrils, planted her hand on her hip, and flashed him the finger. Turning on her heel, she wasted no time following JJ back to the camp.

And her journal.

> Time to find another place to pitch my tent. Dad's giving me the creeps. Gotta talk JJ into going with.

CHAPTER
Thirteen

After relating the story of his shop's vandalism to the Business Chamber members, Jon returned to his seat, trying not to notice the horrified, pitying eyes on him. Outraged murmurs echoed around him. He knew what they were thinking. *Glad it wasn't me.* He'd think the same thing in their shoes.

"Someone was high as a kite," muttered a voice nearby.

"Did you hear one of the RVs caught fire the other night?" Jon didn't recognize the woman speaking. "Two kids were taken to the hospital with smoke inhalation."

A woman behind her asked, "Are they okay?"

The first woman shrugged. "Haven't heard."

"My coffee shop, Ooh Lah Latte, was robbed last month." This came from a woman on the end of Jon's row, who cast him a sympathetic glance. "Considering what you went through, it feels rather petty now. Still, we're getting tired of the thefts and piles of trash everywhere. It's hurting our businesses. What is the county doing about it?"

Another voice chimed in, "They're not building any affordable housing, I can tell you for sure."

Jon turned to see who spoke. Sally, owner of Jon's favorite lunch scene, Sal's Deli, addressed her remark to Bert, the Chamber president. He held up his hands in a don't-look-at-me gesture. "The wheels of government turn slowly, as they say," said Bert. "It's a tough job, balancing compassion with practicality, and a hard sell raising taxes on an already overtaxed county and state."

The atmosphere had grown steadily tenser since the meeting began half an hour ago. The challenges of a room full of opinionated people walking a tightrope between compassion and enabling. In other contexts, Bert, a music store owner, typically came across as genial and easy-going, like most musicians Jon knew. But tonight, the pressure on Bert turned him into someone Jon almost didn't recognize.

Sally tsked. "Are you saying we have no funding to shelter these people? I don't buy it."

Bert's eyes flashed sparks, even as his voice remained politician steady. "If you recall, we voted down the tax measure last year which would have paid for more homeless shelters."

"Then shame on us." Sally sat down and crossed her legs and arms.

Jon had to disagree. He raised his hand. "The measure was too one-size-fits-all. It wouldn't have solved the root causes of homelessness."

Bert gestured in Jon's direction. "I agree with Mr. Paulson. There are as many causes of homelessness as there are homeless people. Even if we build more and bigger shelters, it would only be a partial solution."

Sally tightened her jaw. "What do you mean, a partial solution? We must start somewhere, right?"

"If we don't address the causes of homelessness, it will just go on and on." A few nodded at Bert, who leaned forward, tense and purposeful. "People who lack family connections, even with society in general, are more likely to end up homeless. The experts call it disaffiliation. Kids who've aged out of the foster system also have a higher-than-average risk. Some youths prefer life on the streets to the abusive or unsafe homes they ran from. They lack hope for a better life."

"Most of them are crazies or addicts," someone muttered.

Bert turned to the slick-haired, polo-shirted CEO of Bayside Ironworks. "And they need proper treatment. Sticking them into affordable housing while they're still sick won't fix their problems."

"How did we end up with so many adults who can't adult?" said the first man.

Jon squirmed in discomfort as a finger of guilt needled his spine. Maybe he'd been too hard on those poor unfortunates. His wife was fond of asking herself, "What would Jesus do?" And then attempt to live out the answer.

What would Jesus do if confronted with today's homeless?

A no-brainer. Resolved, he waved his hand until Bert nodded at him. "I propose we ask the County Board what kinds of treatment and housing resources are already at their disposal." Jon shifted, meeting interested faces to the right and left of him. "Do we have enough treatment centers in the area which would get the ones who need it most off the streets? And if we don't, can we get a ballot measure in time for the next election? Not a one-solution measure, but as comprehensive as we can make it."

Another half-hour of back-and-forth until the decision was made to present a three-part proposal to the county and find out if any pending legislation was on the agenda. Jon sat back with a sigh, relieved it was over.

"Jon Paulson?"

He whirled to see a familiar face—the reporter from Marin Mercury who'd interviewed him and Meg last year after a shooting left Meg's son in a coma. The man's lanyard confirmed his identity.

"Steve Davis?" He reached out to shake the reporter's hand. "Good to see you here. I take it you covered the meeting?"

Davis gave Jon's hand a brisk shake. "My editor sent me. I've been assigned a series on the homeless issues in the Bay Area."

"That's great. How long of a series?"

"Two per week for the next three weeks, starting next Monday. I was struck by your story about your vandalized business. And I liked what you said about the multiple causes of homelessness. Mind if I interview you this week?"

Jon hesitated. "Well, it's currently an active police case. I'm not sure I should until it's been solved."

"Yeah, I get that. My editor sent me to live in a homeless camp for a week, and I just got back home two days ago. I got some very revealing interviews. I'll be writing about my experiences, who these people are, and why they have no place to live."

Jon nodded. "Great! I look forward to reading your articles."

Davis saluted. "Tell your wife hello for me," he said, then turned and disappeared out the door.

CHAPTER
Fourteen

The heart asks pleasure first, And then, excuse from pain; And then, those little anodynes That deaden suffering; And then, to go to sleep; And then, if it should be The will of its Inquisitor, The liberty to die.

~Emily Dickinson

Loud, intimidating voices shattered Myla's sleep. She opened her eyes, not sure at first whether this was a dream or reality. As her head cleared, she scrambled to her knees, jostling JJ in the process. "Sorry," she whispered. Judging by his utter lack of motion, he was dead to the world.

A banging outside startled her. "We're clearing the area. You all need to move along." Her heart dropped to her knees. The cops were doing a sweep. They had to move. Again.

Shouts of protest and curses zigzagged through the morning air. Where would they go? And why was Bowie whining? She shook JJ to wake him. "JJ! Wake up!" His body rocked like a lazy canoe, and his arm fell limp to his side. Something about his stillness triggered alarm.

"JJ?" She grabbed his shoulders and shook him harder. Why did he feel so chilled? A memory swept her. Her baby girl—turning cold in her arms.

"JJ!" she screamed, hurling expletives at him as though they would get his attention. "Wake up! Don't you dare do this to me!" He'd only been joking when he mentioned death. Hadn't he? Her heart pummeled her chest, and choking gasps rocketed from her throat.

Bowie stood, his whines morphing to yelps.

"Help!"

She burst from the tent. "Help, somebody. JJ's dead!" A woman cop rushed over and peered in, then knelt next to JJ, holding her finger under his nose, checking his pulse, his eyes, his chest. A grayish pallor tinged JJ's face in the dim tent. Lady Cop clicked her tongue, then pulled out her phone to call someone and have them haul JJ to the morgue. Myla fell next to him and grasped him as tight as her weak, skinny arms could manage. She wouldn't let them put him in a box. No way. She only needed them to revive him. "JJ," she whimpered, over and over. Tears soaked her face, dripping off her chin. Her partner-in-crime. Her only genuine friend. He couldn't be gone. This wasn't real. Any minute she'd wake up from this nightmare and…

"Miss, can you step away from the body, please?"

Myla jumped back at the woman's no-nonsense tone. She wanted to say absolutely not. She wanted to cover JJ with her own body to keep him out of the hole in the ground they planned to put him in. But the uniformed woman sat guard over him, wrinkling her nose at the pungent BO and rotten food odors. Lady Five-O didn't have to be so judgy. She probably lived in a normal home with a normal family. Boring kids with monotonous lives. The kind of life Myla'd always wanted.

"Do you know how it happened?" Lady Cop peered at her with sharp brown eyes. "What's his name? We'll need his next of kin."

Myla, too distraught to speak, shook her head and directed the cop to Mom. She crawled into JJ's empty tent and pawed through his meager possessions with tears raining down her cheeks. She sniffed and wiped her nose with the back of her hand. Where had he kept his stash? Her desperate fingers brushed something cold and hard under the pile of rags he used as a pillow.

The money clip. She pocketed it, then rammed her hands inside his backpack. There. A prescription bottle for OxyContin. She caressed the smooth label, then shook it.

Empty!

Her insides clawed with need. She had to have another pill—soon—to keep the dopesickness at bay. King-Boy was scheduled to make his rounds later today. She sent him a quick, frantic text, then scrambled back outside. Through blurry tears, Myla watched her dearest friend get hauled away—her confidant, her protector. From his appearance, you'd never guess he kept predators from her. His presence beside her prevented Dad and his ilk from ever catching her alone.

Despite the cops' order to vacate the premises, she went back inside her tent and tucked her chin in the cleft of her knees. Rattling sobs, disjointed hiccups, and streams of snot all dripped onto her jeans in one soggy mess.

Who would protect her now?

She sniffed, wiped her nose and cheeks, and whispered into her phone's journal app.

> JJ is gone for good, and I am wrecked. I'm a totaled car. I'm Humpty Dumpty. I'm a smashed-up pumpkin after Halloween. Ain't enough tears in my puny little bod to ever put me back together again.
>
> I miss him already. That oldie song…Love Hurts. Yeppers.

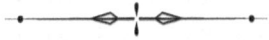

On most Sundays, Meg and Jon enjoyed post-church lunch together either at home or at a local eatery, then took the boat out for a spin in the bay. But today, Meg and Camille's compelling urge to check on the young couple at the homeless camp pulled them into the shop's empty parking lot at one p.m. sharp. As Meg shut off the engine, Camille's sharp gasp made her do a double take.

"What is it?"

Camille stretched her finger to the left. "They're gone."

"Gone?" Sure enough, except for scattered trash, you'd never know tents had lined the sidewalk at the far end of the lot just days ago. "They must have done a sweep!"

"Where could they have gone?"

"They'll probably find another area to camp in. Some of them may have gone to a shelter." Meg started the engine. "We could drive around and look for them if you want."

"Why don't we check further north on the waterfront at some of those empty lots?"

"Good idea." They set off among warehouses and office buildings, in and out of parking lots and loading docks, past seafood restaurants and nightclubs. They scrutinized every grassy expanse. "I just had a bad feeling about those two young people we met last week. BB and JJ."

"What was your bad feeling trying to tell you?"

"It told me they were deep into drug addiction. If they don't get help soon, they'll die." She shuddered and glimpsed a matching tremor from Camille.

"Oh, look." Camille gestured out the open window. "Is this one of them?" A tattered person, stooping under the weight of an overflowing backpack towering higher than her head, shuffled along the sidewalk, pulling a black dog on a leash.

Meg slowed and gawked, unable to believe it was BB who walked the road alone, laden with all her worldly possessions. She held a cell phone, punching out a message.

Without a second thought, Meg pulled to the curb and lowered the passenger window.

BB glanced over, then back to her phone as though she hadn't seen them.

"Hey," Camille called. "Where are you headed?"

BB stopped, radiating suspicion. "No … where special." Her speech stumbled and slurred, and the phone trembled in her hand.

A line from a movie echoed through Meg's head. *Nowhere special. I always wanted to go there.* "We brought more sandwiches, but everybody was gone."

Suspicion morphed into agitation. "The ... the cops m-made us leave."

"Where's the rest of the group?"

BB shrugged and pointed behind her with a shaky finger. Something was obviously wrong with the young woman. Maybe food would help.

"Would you like a sandwich?"

BB stopped and staggered to the window. Her hand shook so hard, she barely managed to shove the phone into her pocket, and then nearly dropped the sandwich Camille held out. "Can ... can I have two? One for me, one for JJ?"

"Of course." As Camille held out a second sandwich, she asked, "Where is JJ?"

"I d-don't ... I don't know." She shook her head vigorously and patted the black Lab. "I think this is ... his dog, Bowie." Sweat dripped from her face, and she wiped her forehead with her soiled sleeve, shoving the second sandwich in her sweater pocket. Her gasps grew frantic as she moved her head side to side. Seeking an escape? A rescue? Another fix?

Camille turned to Meg. "She's either on something," Camille muttered, "or coming down off something."

Meg's stomach twisted into a knot. Leaning over Camille to observe BB's symptoms, she shoved her fingers through her hair and twisted it—her go-to habit when she felt unprepared. The young woman puckered her lips as more sweat drops rolled down her scrunched face. "I ... I ... do you know where JJ is?"

Camille opened the door, and BB jumped back. "Honey, are you okay?"

Before Camille uttered the last word, the young woman swayed, tottered, and crumpled to the ground. The dog, startled, sniffed her and began running in circles, the leash still clutched in her hand.

Camille wasted no time checking on her. Clutching her phone, Meg got out and joined her friend. BB's whole body trembled now, soon morphing to thrashing as though she were suffering from an epileptic seizure. A puddle formed on the seat of BB's holey jeans, and the unmistakable smell of urine crinkled Meg's nose.

Poor girl had wet herself. Meg, her hand shaking almost as bad as BB's, called 911. "I think she's going into withdrawal," she told the operator, heart pounding. Her alarm escalated when BB moaned, a loud, mournful sound like a wounded animal. "Please hurry. She needs help right away."

Helpless to ease BB's discomfort before the ambulance arrived, Meg and Camille held hands and prayed. Then Meg touched BB's wrist and winced at the pulse pounding beneath her fingertips at a hundred miles per hour. She sucked in a steadying breath and launched another arrow prayer to heaven, pleading with the Lord to bring help quickly.

Two minutes later, the ambulance rushed in. Unable to give the paramedics any information on BB's real name or address, Meg returned to the car while Camille chatted with one of the crew.

Moments later, Camille put the dog in the back seat of Meg's car and plopped in front. Meg opened her mouth, but Camille plowed on. "They told me they're taking her to St. Vincent's. It has one of the best detox units in the area." Her active hands punctuated each word. "Let's go check on her tomorrow, okay?"

"If the hospital allows it. And, um, why is the dog in my back seat?"

"I'm taking him home with me. What did she say his name was?"

"Bowie. As in David Bowie."

"Ah. Seems like a good dog, other than being a little on the skinny side. Bill and I will fatten him right up."

"I know you will, girlfriend." Meg started the engine and headed for home, quivering a little inside at the agony of withdrawal. She hadn't witnessed it before today and didn't wish to ever again. "Whew, that was intense. Which makes me even more convinced—whoever is supplying those poor people with drugs ought to be locked up for the rest of their lives."

CHAPTER

Fifteen

Meg relaxed in Noelle Marquette's break room, sipping her ten o'clock coffee and clutching the morning newspaper. Recognizing the reporter's byline, she set her coffee down, riveted to the words in front of her. This must be the homeless series by Steve Davis Jon had told her about.

THE MARIN MERCURY

THAT HOMELESS LIFE
by Steve Davis

PART 1 OF A 6-PART SERIES

You approach the tattered tent city cautiously, careful to avoid the needles and human waste on the sidewalk. You notice cars packed to the gills, in varying degrees of degeneration, parked haphazardly on the sidewalk. Graffiti covers most available surfaces. Shabbily dressed people mill about with apparently nothing productive to do, and you can't help wondering, who are these people, and how did they end up living like third-world citizens here in the wealthiest nation on Planet Earth?

In this six-part series, I tell the story of how I experienced life for myself as an undercover resident in one of Marin County's many homeless camps, whose location will remain confidential.

It's no secret that the homeless sweeps in San Francisco have displaced many homeless citizens and have spilled over into our communities here in Marin County. Last week, a Sausalito businessman's shop was severely vandalized shortly after a homeless community set up camp across the parking lot. His business is virtually ruined, and he fears he has lost everything. Although he has no solid proof, he can't help wondering if someone, or a few someones, from the camp might have had something to do with it.

Before you judge him for being "judgmental," let's look at some history and some stats. In San Francisco over the past decade, wherever homelessness increased, so did petty thefts and vandalism against nearby businesses. Many of these businesses were forced to invest in state-of-the-art security or move away. When businesses moved to safer sites, the empty spaces left behind encourage even more crime and vagrancy.

I spoke with Marin County spokesperson Anne Jaynes-Bateman about the proliferating homeless camps in the area. "We simply don't have enough beds for all the people who need them," she told me. "The numbers of houseless persons are exploding far faster than we can build, which leaves us with year-long waiting lists at our existing shelters and low-income housing units. At the last census, more than a thousand unsheltered county residents lived here, despite our significant investments in supportive housing over the last six years. Just last year, we distributed over $35 million in local, state, and federal funds for emergency rental assistance."

When asked what the county's plans were for providing shelter for those currently unsheltered, Ms. Jaynes-Bateman said, "The process is incredibly slow, unfortunately. If we could speed it up, we certainly would. From the time architectural plans are drawn up, contractors are hired and permits approved, it can be up to two years before the buildings are ready to be lived in. Then, of course, we have to have the proper support services within access, such as ongoing rehab services and education, pharmaceutical services where residents can get their meds—all the usual stuff. None of these things happens overnight."

I asked her what county residents should expect. "Just be patient. We need everyone to understand getting people off the streets and into stable housing is going to take time."

Today's article attempts to answer the question, who are these people forced to live on the streets? Where are they coming from, and why are they here?

The many reasons for homelessness are complex. But from this reporter's research, we found the following situations most common.

1.   Low-income workers priced out of the housing market by ever-increasing rents. Some of these people have less than a high school education and may work more than one minimum wage job just to make ends meet, which is not enough to afford rent in much of the Bay Area. They may end up "couch-surfing" among friends and family. If that option ends, some people find it easiest to just set up a tent on a sidewalk or park their car at a curb and pay no rent at all. To combat this, the county has an eviction moratorium and a rent freeze in place. So it comes as a bit of a surprise to learn a sizable percentage of people living on the street or in their cars are employed. This is the situation "Irene," who grew up in Vallejo, finds herself in. She works four days a week, eight hours a day, at a local fast-food restaurant. After her last rent increase, she decided she and her two middle-school kids would be fine living in her Ford van, which she parks near a vacant lot two blocks from her employer. The three of them sleep on mattresses in the back, and a school bus picks up the kids each morning. Once they're on their way, Irene walks to work. When the kids are dropped off after school, they hang out at the restaurant until Mom's shift is done. "Works for us, at least for now," Irene claims. "I keep

telling my girls, 'This is only temporary.' I'm saving money by not paying rent, and maybe by this time next year, we'll be in an actual apartment."

2.   Abuse and/or violence. I met a few moms with young ones who had escaped abusive relationships. They had no one to take them in; their Significant Others had forced them to break ties with friends and family. They felt they had no choice but to live in their cars with their kids. "It's safer for me and the kids out here on the street," one mom, who asked to remain anonymous, told me. When she was informed of the locations of women's shelters, she told me they were all full, with waiting lists a mile long.

3.   Recently released parolees. True, halfway houses are available, but, like most public services, we simply don't have enough of them. Many inmates learn trades while incarcerated and sometimes have jobs waiting for them. Despite the fact these ex-cons could afford housing, many landlords hesitate to rent to them. After many years in prison, they may gain freedom only to find all their former life connections broken. With doors slamming everywhere they go, they might wander for miles, sometimes across state lines, seeking the support they need, but too often ending up on the street…only to eventually re-offend.

4.   The mentally ill. These people are the visible ones, the ones most of us think of when we visualize the homeless. But why are they on the street and not in a care facility? In the '50s and '60s, a backlash from the appalling conditions of "insane asylums" led to a trend of emphasizing community treatment over institutionalization. Over time, more and more mental health institutions closed, and patients deemed

not a threat to themselves, or others, were released, with the caveat that community mental health clinics would bear the burden for their treatment. Problem is, federal funding dried up, and state and local governments were expected to assume responsibility for funding. In the '80s, laws began limiting states from committing people against their will, thus the trend of "deinstitutionalization" began. Mental hospitals emptied out, while at the same time, communities began offering tax breaks to owners of low-income housing as incentives to gentrify. Housing for low-income families began to dry up, and as gentrification became more popular in many cities, more individuals and families became displaced. Funding didn't stretch far enough to cover the immense need, and with not enough community facilities ready to step in, many of those people have ended up on the streets. Many mentally ill men and women take their meds inconsistently or have trouble obtaining them, either due to lack of access to pharmacies or lack of funds. Sometimes, after a mental health crisis, they are taken to a local emergency room, where they are treated but often released without a plan. I talked to a fellow I'll call "Gregory," who has battled schizophrenia since his teen years. He's now thirty-five, grew up in the area, and has been in and out of treatment for years. Today, he lives in a brand-new tent in a small community of about ten other tents set up in a field. "I try to remember to take my meds," he says, "but I've been known to forget my refills. When I run out, sometimes I black out and come to days later, with no idea what day it is. But we look out for each other here." He gestures toward the other tents. "They don't let me get too far gone." He drinks wine to quiet the voices in his head, but it doesn't always work.

5.   The addict. The stereotypical homeless guy, the one our parents warned us against. But these days, a new type of addict rules the streets—those hooked on the street drugs meth, opioids, heroin, and even fentanyl, a dangerous new hybrid drug which can shut down your system in minutes. Today's addicts aren't your typical alcoholic or wino. They're enslaved to a deadly habit which can also endanger those around them, especially if the drug is meth or OxyContin. We've heard horror stories of children being raised by meth-addicted parents. Even more horrific tales of high schoolers experimenting with fentanyl, with tragic results. We've heard much about the terrible Oxy addiction epidemic sweeping our nation and the big pharmaceutical companies pushing it with misleading claims. And the doctors who are in the drug companies' pockets. While researching for this article, I met young people who'd been prescribed the drug as pre-teens or teens after an injury, and, tragically, the drug eventually took over their lives. They often end up dropping out of school, out of family life, and out of society. These are kids who may have been raised in stable homes, whose parents trusted their doctor when he or she encouraged their teen to take this painkiller. Parents and kids who never dreamed of addiction in their future. When addiction snatches hold of someone, it rarely lets go without a bloody, knock-down-drag-out fight. Many addicts have burned bridges with family and friends, and soon the street becomes their only option. Why don't drug addicts get treatment, you may ask. I found a young man camped in the backyard of a "zombie" house (a foreclosed property deteriorating from lack of owner upkeep). He rode a bus here from Denver after hearing rumors of how "homeless-friendly" San Francisco is. I assume he means a higher level of tolerance. He admitted heroin is his drug of

choice and fears the terrible withdrawals his friends tell him about. It's what keeps him from a treatment facility. And all their "ridiculous" rules. (The following quote is not verbatim since this is a family-friendly newspaper.) "You gotta stay clean, do a bunch of dumb *** chores, check in super early, all that *** crap. No thanks. Living in a tent is better than someone always watching you and telling you what *** *** to do. They ain't the boss of me."

6.   Juvenile runaways. By far the most heart-wrenching of the bunch. Kids as young as fourteen are camping on the streets, their faces hard beyond their years, their innocence long gone. I tried to talk to some, but only one agreed. I got it. They're in hiding and want to stay that way. The one who let me interview him gave his name as Mick. He claimed he hitchhiked down here from Vancouver, Washington, after he ran away from his foster home. "Were they abusive?" I asked him. "Naw, not really, just always on my case about stupid ***. They had, like, two other foster kids and three bio kids. I was invisible anyway, so one of the other foster kids and I took off for Frisco. Figured they'd never notice we were gone." He'd landed in the foster system when he was ten after a relative noticed welts on his legs. Turned out his stepdad had been whipping him frequently. Many foster kids end up on the streets, Mick told me. After probing further, I got the feeling so many of them ran because they were abused and neglected, and by the time they ended up in a stable home, the damage was done. Some of them never get the life skills they need to transition successfully into adulthood.

In fact, the common denominator among these six types of homeless persons seems to be former foster kids. I don't have any hard and fast statistics to prove it, but Mick claims about one in four addicts, parolees, and runaways are people who've gone through the foster care system.

Folks, we are failing our children in so many ways. And I saw plenty of evidence this week.

Next up: Boots on the Ground – Life in a Homeless Camp

Meg shuddered as she set the paper down, her eyes moist.

"Imagine being one of those poor, neglected kids," she said to the person whose shadow blocked the doorway.

Meg's boss, immaculate as usual, cleared her throat and entered the room, her heels clattering on the brown tile floor. "Meg, there you are." Sylvana's voice gave no sign she'd heard Meg. "I expected you back at your desk by now."

Meg sprang to her feet. The wall clock showed 10:20 already. "I'm so sorry. This article distracted me, and I didn't notice the time." She needed to disarm her boss. Holding out the paper, she said, "Here, read this. It's an excellent article on homelessness. It even refers to my husband's shop robbery I mentioned last week."

After a long moment, Sylvana took it. Unable to read her boss's professional countenance, Meg hurried back to her desk, hoping the article would make Sylvana forget Meg's sloppy time management.

Some things were more important than promptness.

CHAPTER

Sixteen

A poor torn heart, a tattered heart, That sat it down to rest, Nor noticed that the ebbing day Flowed silver to the west... The angels, happening that way, This dusty heart espied; Tenderly took it up from toil, And carried it to God.

– Emily Dickinson

"Honey, that girl's withdrawals were the most agonizing thing I've ever seen." Meg put down her soup spoon and waited for Jon to reply. From the kitchen window, she watched the fog roll in over the bay. Soon it would sweep over their Sausalito neighborhood and plunge them into semidarkness. Meg didn't think she'd ever tire of the sight, despite having lived in Marin County all her life. She loved living here in Jon's white stucco cottage on Bayview Avenue, with its pebbled backyard overlooking rugged Angel Island. In spring, the wild rose bushes Jon's ex-wife had planted years ago wrapped their light perfume over his front yard like a sweet blanket.

"I'm sorry you had to witness it." Jon, across the dinner table, clanked his spoon on the ceramic bowl. "Kudos to you and Camille for your fast-acting response."

"We plan to drop by the hospital tomorrow and hope they'll tell us how she's doing."

"I doubt they will, due to HIPAA laws."

"We're going to try. Want to come along?"

"No, I have an appointment with the insurance agent. I also need to follow up with Officer Lee to see if they've made progress locating Myla Delaney."

"Who's Myla Delaney?" asked Tanner, slurping another spoonful of clam chowder.

"Someone who used to work at your dad's shop." Meg had a fuzzy recollection of the young woman on the few occasions she'd visited Jon, but never got a good look at her face.

"Tanner, you might remember her from last summer when you worked there. Dark brown hair about yea long." Jon jabbed a spot midway down his arm. "Worked in the office."

"Oh, yeah. The chick Connor liked."

"I didn't realize your brother liked her."

"He most def had the hots for her."

"He did, huh? Now I understand why he recommended her for the job."

The glow outside turned dusky silver, and Meg turned on the lights. "Jon, how did your son know Myla?"

"From high school. I'll call him after dinner to see if he's talked to her recently." Jon finished his last bite. "Tanner, got homework tonight?"

"Yeah. Sophomore English."

"Go work on it while Meg and I talk."

Tanner complied after he emptied his chowder bowl and clanked it into the sink.

She shifted on the bench seat and asked, "What makes you and Patti think Myla's the perp?"

"Patti recognized her manga art. Plus, whoever broke into the shop was someone familiar with the place. They knew how to avoid tripping the security light on. They knew when the custodian would arrive. They knew the alarm code."

Meg cupped her chin in her hand. "What I want to know is, who helped her?"

"Yes, the big unknown."

"Does it shock you a former employee would do this?"

"At first, it did. But then I started remembering stuff. Toward the end of her tenure with us, she was putting out a bad vibe. Not at first, though. She was my son's friend, and he vouched for her. Early on, she seemed cooperative, kind of quiet, a solid employee. Then she got pregnant and had a stillborn baby. After a month, we welcomed her back, but she was never the same. She started coming in late or calling in sick more than normal."

"Oh, poor, poor girl. Grief can really affect a person."

"Patti would find cash missing from the cash box, and occasionally an employee would report something missing."

"Like what?"

"Tools, mainly. Some of the more valuable ones can be sold on Amazon for a decent sum."

"Did you have any proof it was her?"

"Nothing solid. But then her reports got sloppy, and she started committing more and more errors. The boneheaded kind, like her mind had gone bye-bye. Patti and I talked, and after some internet searching on signs of drug abuse, we realized she was showing all the signs. So we sent her to get tested. She failed."

"How long ago was this?"

"Three, four months or so."

"How would she have been able to get into the shop? Did she still have a key?"

He carried his dishes to the sink. "I've been thinking about that. She couldn't have used a key because Patti collected it from her."

"Could she have copied it?"

"No. It was a fob, which isn't duplicable. However, we didn't change the alarm code after she left—my mistake, as it turns out—so she'd only need an unlocked door. And when is the door unlocked outside of business hours?"

"When the custodian is there?"

"Bingo. She's familiar with his routine. Let's say she times it exactly to sneak in behind him. She brings along her partner, someone strong enough to inflict great damage. They hide somewhere until the custodian is done. He sets the alarm and shuts the door. Then she keys in the alarm code she still remembers, and they go crazy. They ransack the shop, she decorates the boats, he totals them." Jon's jaw hardened as the memory stirred up fresh anger. "Then she resets the alarm, and they skedaddle."

"Sounds convincing, honey. But what would her motive be?"

"Easy drug money. And revenge."

"Revenge?"

"She yelled at me on her way out. 'You're going to pay for this.' I won't repeat the other words she shouted."

Once the dishes were loaded, Jon took his phone into the master bedroom to call his oldest son, who lived in Berkeley and attended Cal. He and Meg perched on the edge of the bed as the phone rang.

"Yeah, Dad?"

"Hey." After they'd gotten the small talk out of the way, Jon got to the point. "Do you remember Myla Delaney?"

"Um, yeah, sure. What about her?"

"When was the last time you saw or talked to her?"

Connor made a scoffing noise. "The last time I saw her was eons ago."

"How many eons ago? A year? Last week?"

"Months. Why?"

"Some unfinished business regarding her employment, but nobody seems to know where she is. I hoped you could help."

"I tried staying in touch with her after she started working for you, but she quit replying to my texts. Eventually, I gave up. What happened to her job with you?"

"I had to let her go a few months ago."

"Seriously? But why?"

"I can't really go into it due to confidentiality reasons …"

"Well, now you really got me curious."

"Think you could track her down for me?"

"Possibly. I think we're still Facebook friends. Hold on a minute while I check."

Clicks and mutters from the other end, then, "Looks like she deactivated her account."

Meg rubbed Jon's drooping shoulders as he thanked his son and secured Connor's promise to keep his eyes and ears open for Myla's whereabouts. "If you manage to locate her, I'll buy you a boat for your twenty-first birthday. A Phleet."

"Wow, really? I love Phleet boats. This must be super important. I'll ask around—see what I can do."

"I appreciate it."

Meg massaged the back of Jon's neck as he said goodbye. "You found the perfect motivator."

He took her hand. "I have another idea in case Operation Phleet doesn't work out." He turned to face her. "Your son-in-law. He has access to all kinds of databases. And, since Lee and Jackson are taking their time …" He tapped his phone. "I know Ken will get right on it."

CHAPTER

Seventeen

There are things of which I may not speak; There are dreams that cannot die; There are thoughts that make the strong heart weak, And bring a pallor into the cheek. And a mist before the eye. And the words of that fatal song Come over me like a chill: "A boy's will is the wind's will, And the thoughts of youth are long, long thoughts."

~Henry Wadsworth Longfellow, MY LOST YOUTH

Tanner Paulson crept back to his room, his dad and stepmother's conversation echoing through his head. Sure, he shouldn't have hovered nearby, eavesdropping, but at least he'd learned something valuable.

That girl Connor liked had vandalized Dad's shop. Or so his dad believed. And she'd had help. But who had helped her? Most likely, the guy he'd seen looking in the windows. Should he tell Dad his suspicions? But what if he did and he turned out to be mistaken? He could be in terrible, serious trouble if he got this one wrong.

For now, best to keep his hunch to himself and let the police handle it. Still, his gut twisted, and something snaked up his spine. He shivered. His mom would say a goose walked over his grave.

He needed to think about something else, so he checked his phone for messages and found a text from his friend Ethan Koningson. *Comin over soon for an edible?*

Finally! A grin stretched across Tanner's features. *Yep, BRT. Found a site u will like. GirlzXXX, you sonuva Paulson*
CU, u sonuva Koningson

They'd played that silly name game since Ethan moved here four years ago, and Tanner's dad taught them substitute swearwords. He tucked his homework folder, plastered with Golden Gate High School logos, into the crook of his arm, then found his dad in his room with Meg kneeling beside the bed in their familiar prayer ritual. His dad looked up, a question in the lines of his forehead, and Tanner gestured in the general direction of Ethan's apartment complex, holding up the folder. His dad nodded and gave the okay sign. Tanner breathed a sigh of relief, amazed at how easy it was to fool his dad into believing he and Ethan would be working on their English assignment together.

He walked a block to the main boulevard and entered La Cienega Apartment's courtyard, the canopy of willow trees providing welcome relief from the sun's heat. Unit ten sat on the north end. Ethan's mom and Mr. Bunkert, Ethan's stepdad, were watching TV and hardly acknowledged Tanner's entrance. He slipped into Ethan's room. "I wanna see that site."

Ethan chuckled and turned the laptop Tanner's way. "See, I told you it was good."

"Dame!" he said, another of his dad's alternate swearwords. A strange mixture of delight and shame crept up Tanner's spine, but he kept scrolling through the images. His dad would kill him if he knew what they were up to. But maybe Dad shouldn't have put so many parental controls on his phone and laptop. If he hadn't, Tanner might not have been so curious about what his dad was trying to hide from him.

Ethan's stepdad, Mitch, was way cooler than his own dad, letting Ethan and his brother Dwyer do whatever they wanted. Maybe because he wasn't their real dad. Mitch paid his biological daughter, Natalie, a lot more attention than he did his stepsons. Ethan's real dad died when he was a baby, and his mom married a doctor who adopted her two sons, but the marriage didn't last. When Ethan was ten, she met

Mitch. But Mitch Bunkert was no Jon Paulson, not to mention several steps down from a doctor. Poor Ethan—having to move from a nice home into a cramped apartment. He couldn't understand what Ethan's mom had been thinking. But if she hadn't married Mitch and become downwardly mobile, Tanner wouldn't have met his ultra-cool friend.

"Let's go to the city this weekend," Ethan muttered. "I know where we can find some girls."

"Yeah?" Tanner breathed, a thrill of fright lurching his heart. Real live girls, who could make a man out of him?

He scrolled some more, and Ethan handed him a yellow cube which resembled Jello. "Here's the edible I told you about. It's only ten milligrams of THC, and it'll help you sleep. And your old man won't smell it on you when you get home."

He'd never had an edible before. He'd heard they tasted like gummy worms. "Where'd you get it?"

"Dwyer."

As if he'd been summoned, Ethan's older brother stuck his head in the room. "Did I hear my name, Perv?" He turned his attention to Tanner. "Hey, Shortcake. You're gonna like that weed."

Dwyer was the coolest guy on the block, which also made him the scariest. You didn't want to get on Dwyer's bad side. Tanner popped the morsel in his mouth at the same time Ethan did. The raves about its taste didn't do it justice. This tasted better than gummy worms.

At first, he didn't notice anything different. Then the images on the laptop screen started drifting and swaying. Tanner felt himself float outside his body, then drift aimlessly, his feet flailing, unable to grip the floor. His heart raced as panic built in his chest.

Hovering inches above the floor, he flailed his arms, seeking solid ground. Why couldn't he get back to himself? What was happening to him? He'd lost himself, and he didn't know how to get back. He had split in two and…

"Du-u-u-u-ude…" A voice from a horror film undulated nearby, intensifying his nightmare. *Please let me wake up soon.*

Another voice yelled, louder this time. "What's happening to me?" Then he realized it was his own.

"Du-u-u-u-ude … Chi-i-i-i-lll." Reality slapped him back to Ethan's room, where his friend shook him, rocking his body as violently as if he'd jumped into a tidal wave machine. Countless moments passed. Rocking. Floating. It could've been two minutes. Or ten. Or thirty. Time, space, and matter lost all meaning.

"You … better … get … home, dude." Dwyer's voice came at him like an auditory strobe light. "You're freaking out."

Somehow, he found himself on Ethan's front porch. Next thing he knew, he stood—still in an eerie out-of-body state—on his own porch. At least, it looked like his house, but the walls kept moving and shifting as if it were a stage set.

"Son … what's … wrong?"

His dad's face loomed large, growing larger by the second. With a whimper, Tanner dashed inside, yelling. "Help me!" His voice reverberated around him, bouncing off walls and ceiling.

He sought anything familiar, anything to ground him, but things kept moving around. His room! He needed the security of his own private space. Then maybe he'd feel normal again.

Tanner fell back on his bed and watched the ceiling fan spin. Except it wasn't on. The whole room spun around him while he stayed motionless on his bed. Dad and Meg followed him in, their features distorted, their eyes set lopsided in their heads. His rational mind knew it was an illusion. Yet this feeling … this high … it sucked. Why did his peers think weed was so great? Why hadn't he been more careful? Why had he agreed to try something he knew was risky?

God must be punishing him for his stupidity. He turned his face into his pillow and wailed.

CHAPTER

Eighteen

Myla was dreaming.

Or else she was dying.

How to explain this terrible sickness, far worse than the worst case of flu she could imagine? She was trapped in a horrible prison cell where the vomiting went on and on until she must be puking up her entire insides.

At this rate, she'd disintegrate into nonexistence.

Someone kept applying a cool compress to her face and whispering soothing words. "Hush now, you'll be okay. Just a little longer, and this will be all over."

Was she delivering Lula all over again? But how was it possible?

When she wasn't hugging bedpans, something clawed her bones. Only Oxy could make it stop.

She needed a fix in the worst way. "Let me out of here!" she screamed, but someone held her down. She thrashed, then felt a needle prick. *Finally. Bring on the Oxy.*

Calm descended, and she slept.

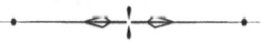

A surreal cloud fell over Meg as she watched her stepson thrashing and moaning. She searched Jon's frantic expression, seeking reassurance, but found none. Her heartbeat raced. What had happened to him?

Jon sat on the bed and held out his hand for his son to cling to. "Tanner, you need to tell me what's going on. Did you have something to eat at Ethan's?"

Nodding, Tanner seemed to shrink into himself. "I had an edible. Everyone says they're no big deal."

"An edible? You mean marijuana?" Jon turned to Meg and said in an undertone, "Apparently, I erred when I let him visit Ethan tonight." Addressing Tanner, he added, "So you and Ethan weren't really working on homework."

Tanner only scrunched his face tighter, his frightened gaze clinging to Jon's. Meg's tension rose. She knew marijuana these days held more potency and posed more danger than the pot from her own youth.

Jon stood. "Do you need to go to Urgent Care?"

Tanner shook his head. "It's supposed to wear off."

"When I warned you about the dangers of drugs, this is what I was talking about."

"I know." Tanner lurched, then heaved upward. "I gotta puke." He jumped from the bed and staggered to the hallway like a drunk man but rammed the doorjamb instead. He finally maneuvered himself to the bathroom, and Meg and Jon listened to him retch. "Bye bye, clam chowder," Jon muttered. "Honey, do you mind staying here while I talk with Ethan's oblivious parents?"

"I wish we both could go."

"I do too."

Tanner flew from the bathroom and plopped back onto his bed, holding his stomach and groaning. Meg assured Jon she'd tend to Tanner, so he left. She sat beside him and whispered soothing words, dabbing his cheeks and brow with a cool cloth as though he were her own son.

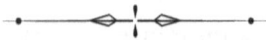

Jon pounded on the Bunkert's front door. Rustling noises and loud voices carried through the open window screen. He heard Mr.

Bunkert yell, "I told you to quit wasting all that printer paper. What is this crap?"

Dwyer's voice whined, "It's for work, I told you."

"For work, my … Doesn't that pot shop have a printer?"

Jon rang the doorbell as he recalled Dwyer worked at the cannabis dispensary down on Second. A door slammed somewhere inside at the same time the front door flew open. Mitch Bunkert stood there, thick arms folded, big feet ten inches apart like the ex-Marine he was. "Hey. Whatcha need?"

Jon stuck out his hand. "Good evening, Mitch."

Mitch took the hand and shook. "How are ya?"

"Good. I'm here about Tanner. I believe he was over here earlier?"

"Yeah, he was. Didn't see much of him till he ran out of here like the devil was chasing him."

I think he was.

Mitch shifted from foot to foot as if the subject made him nervous. "Asked Ethan what was going on. He said Tanner felt sick and went home. Is he okay?"

"Mind if I come in?"

Mitch held the door wide with a sweeping motion. Jon stepped in, struck by the TV volume dominating the home's airwaves. Struck by the lack of movement anywhere else. Beth Bunkert and their daughter, Natalie, sank into the sofa, staring motionless at a Netflix show. But where was Ethan?

Jon faced Mitch, his jaw firmed. "Your son gave Tanner an edible tonight. He had a bad reaction to it. You might want to have a chat with him."

A defensive expression tightened Bunkert's face, and he resumed his ex-Marine stance. "I assume you'll have a chat with yours."

"Already did. I've warned him over and over of the dangers of messing with drugs."

A forced grin twisted Bunkert's mouth. "You know how boys are. If you forbid something, they want to try it even more. I'm sure you remember what it's like to be a teenager."

"But if you educate them on the danger, they're less likely to experiment."

Mitch reached for the doorknob. "Point taken. Need to get back to what I was doing. I'm sorry your son had a bad reaction."

He stuck out a meaty hand, and Jon pumped it once. "Have a good evening," Jon said as he turned and left.

Meg met him at their front door. "How did it go?"

Jon shook his head and thrust a thumb in the direction of the Bunkert apartment. "With parents like them, it's no wonder we have so many messed up kids. How's Tanner?"

"He seems calmer but still very stoned. Hopefully, he sleeps it off tonight."

Groans reached them from the back bedroom. Jon, trailed by Meg, rushed in. Tanner, flat on his back, pointed at the ceiling and moaned. "What are those things on the ceiling?"

Meg laid a hand on Jon's arm. "Should we take him to Urgent Care?"

He squeezed her hand as he watched his son. "Yes. Better make sure nothing worse is going on. Tanner, get up, son. We're taking you to the doctor."

CHAPTER

Nineteen

Life treads on life, and heart on heart; We press too close in church and mart To keep a dream or grave apart.

~Elizabeth Barrett Browning

Meg's clenched muscles slowly relaxed as she and Jon watched Tanner awaken after sleeping off his high. Last night at Community Medical Center, the ER physician, Dr. Jenkins, had given Tanner a sedative and assured them he would be okay in the morning. "Now that recreational marijuana is legal in California," he'd said, "I'm not surprised how many teenagers end up here, having overdone it." He ran a hand over his gelled hair. "They either don't know their limitations, or they don't take the risks seriously." He nodded down at Tanner, whose peaceful expression belied his earlier turmoil. "His system might be more sensitive than others his age. Hopefully, he'll learn from this."

"I have no doubt he will." Jon's solemn voice had cracked with emotion. And exhaustion.

Now Tanner rubbed his eyes and blinked at them.

"How are you feeling, son?"

He sat up. "Okay, sort of." He eased himself off the bed and stood still, assessing his condition. Steady on his feet. No wobbles. He moved his head from side to side. "My head feels normal again. I suppose I have to go to school now."

"In light of what could have happened to you," Jon said, "I'm thankful for a positive outcome."

"Yeah, I guess."

Tanner's short-term nightmare had ended, but her husband's would continue. He'd temporarily closed the shop and planned to spend the day dealing with insurance red tape. While he navigated a horrifying reality, she headed off to work. She wished they hadn't had to rush off. She'd love to go back to bed for more snuggles and marital love with her husband. Instead, she'd settle for a long goodbye kiss and anticipate a romantic night later. With a smile hovering on her lips, she rushed into the kitchen for a coffee refill. Kassidy would be here any moment to accompany Meg on her long commute into the city. The thought of her impending grandbaby brought a spring to her step and sent her back to her room for a final makeup-and-outfit inspection and the long goodbye kiss with Jon.

The doorbell rang, and she hurried to the door. "Sid!" She hugged her daughter-in-law. "Soon to be Mommy!"

Kassidy's still-flat belly belied her declaration. Meg couldn't imagine her frail frame expanding far enough to produce a baby in seven months.

Kassidy grinned as she stepped inside. Her luminous gray eyes danced. "And not a hint of morning sickness, so far."

Meg retrieved her black cardigan from the coat rack, and she and Kassidy made their way to the garage. "I didn't either when I was pregnant with Rich. But I did with Linzee. Wonder if you've got a baby boy growing in there."

She turned the radio to their favorite Christian station as they set out. They'd almost reached the bridge when a question popped from Meg's mouth. "How is Rich these days? Seems like it's been a long time since we've talked. He takes forever to respond to my texts and doesn't ever return my calls. I've given up leaving voice mails."

Her hands tightened on the wheel. Kassidy's porcelain complexion had grown even paler.

"Did I hit a nerve?"

Kassidy paused, her mouth downturned. "I'm a little worried about him. Did you know he's on Oxy?"

Meg gasped. "No. He never said anything to me. I only knew he was struggling with pain and tremors. When I texted him about treatment, he was very vague."

"I love him to death, but I don't want to be married to a drug addict. Or raise a child with an addicted father."

"He's showing signs of addiction?"

A tear trembled on Kassidy's cheek. "I'm not sure. He sometimes seems out of it when I get home. Or I'll notice his eyes look kind of glazed over." She heaved a huge sigh. "I think he's really down on himself since he hasn't been working."

"Is one of his doctors prescribing them?" She tensed, almost afraid to hear the answer.

"Yes, it's a legal prescription. But it seems like his doctor would be trying to wean him off them by now. I did some research and learned Oxy usage is usually closely monitored."

Meg sucked in a sharp breath. She'd raised Rich to avoid drugs, and he'd done a good job staying clean, or so she'd thought. The shooting injury from last year which had turned their world inside out … was its life-altering power still imposing itself? God's grace had reached down into the darkness, performing miracles of healing and bringing peace to her and Jon's troubled hearts. But had it been a mere temporary fix?

"Maybe you could call his doctor and find out what the plan is. Tell him your worries."

"I've been thinking the same."

"Please let me know what you find out. If they're willing to tell you."

Thoughts swirled through Meg's head as she turned into the parking garage. Visions of opioid addicts with gaunt frames and pockmarked skin sent a shudder through her. She could still see the young man from the homeless camp, JJ. Could her son end up a walking corpse, like JJ, desperate for a fix, with no home but the streets? Turning to theft to fund his habit? Or would she become an enabler, unable to turn him over to the consequences of his choices?

Hot waves of alarm pummeled her heart as she and Kassidy neared Noelle Marquette, the high-end department store where she'd worked for more than twelve years as a Merchandiser. She couldn't let Kassidy see her distress. She had to be strong for her. "Are you two attending church these days?"

"Rarely. He sleeps late most mornings."

Meg's heart sunk. Rich shouldn't expect his life to turn around if he wasn't connecting to God, the ultimate Transformer.

Rich groaned, hating the house's emptiness and his wife's absence. Another tedious, pain-filled day stretched ahead of him. Nothing appealed to him anymore—TV, video games, social media. But because he had nothing else to do, he sprawled on the sofa in the TV room and grabbed the game controller for Mario Party.

He clicked on his avatar name, RichMan245, and waited for the action to start. Devonator and SofaTater soon joined. Although strangers, they made him feel as though two friends had come to visit.

His head was killing him. The Oxy didn't work as well today. On the one hand, he needed to take another dose. On the other hand, if the pain didn't clobber him, the Oxy's aftereffects very well could.

The doorbell rang, followed by two quick knocks.

The noise rattled his head, and he groaned, slamming the controller to the sofa. He heaved himself up, then peeked through the eyehole and saw Jake, his old friend from next door.

Rich cracked the door open. "Dude. What up?"

Jake pushed inside. "Didn't you get my text?"

"Your text?" When had he last checked his phone? He patted his jeans pockets. No phone. He must have left it in the bedroom. "No."

"I told you I was home for a few days to help my mom and dad move and asked if I could come over."

Rich ran a hand down his face. "Sorry. I haven't checked my phone yet."

Jake made himself at home on the sofa. "You look like crap, dude. You've lost a ton of weight too. What's up with you?"

Way to put a guy on the defensive. "Did you come over here to insult me?"

"No, sorry. Just wanted to say hi and see how you're doing."

"Doing fine. I'm gonna be a dad in about seven months." No need to mention his misgivings about how he would support a child when his disability barely covered the bills.

"Yo. Congratulations, bro."

"Thanks." He sensed an intensified scrutiny from Jake.

"Really, how are you doing? Last time I saw you, you'd just finished physical therapy. Looks like it worked. You seem to be moving around just fine."

"Yeah, it worked great."

Jake indicated the TV where the paused video game waited. "Want a partner?"

"Sure." Rich sprawled in the easy chair, and they manipulated the controls for a few minutes. After a winning move, Jake let out a holler, and the sound hammered Rich's head.

"Knock it off!" Rich clutched his head as if to protect it from noisy invaders.

Jake put out his hand like a shield. "Whoa, dude. Are you hungover?"

Rich shook his head. "No. Just a headache. I've had them for months. It really sucks."

"Don't you take anything for it?"

"Yeah, the doc has me on Oxy. But sometimes they don't work."

"Better be careful with those. I have a cousin who got hooked on 'em. He lost everything. They ruined his life."

"I'm careful. It's just…the pain never really goes away."

"I feel for you, man."

They picked up the controllers, but his friend's warning rang through his head as they resumed the game. *He lost everything.*

He'd already lost everything when he got shot. And step by step, he got his life back. Almost.

Inside, he gave a silent shrug. What could be worse than being in a coma for three weeks, waking up, and realizing you couldn't walk or talk? At least with pain pills, he didn't lose his faculties. And he gained a pain-free glow.

Twenty

Jon picked up the morning edition of the local paper as he sipped his latte at Sal's Deli. Steve's article dominated the front page.

THE MARIN MERCURY

THAT HOMELESS LIFE
by Steve Davis

PART 2 OF A 6-PART SERIES

With a scruffy beard (which elicited raised eyebrows from my wife and daughter), wearing my oldest, most ragged pieces of clothing I can find in the back of my closet, I sneak into the homeless camp in the early morning hours. There's just enough dawning light to see what I'm doing, so I dig my tent out of my backpack and find a spare plot of grass to set it up. The camp stretches along a freeway onramp for about an eighth of a mile, and I observe the cars entering the freeway. My old Dodgers cap is pulled low over my eyes, and I don't think anyone who knows me would recognize me if they happened to drive by.

Soon my tent is set up, and the noises around me are telling me the inhabitants of the tents beside mine are waking up. I smell something cooking and realize I should have brought my camp stove. I'll have to figure out a way to get it from home. My orders were, live on the streets for a week, don't go home, don't come to the office. Until your week is up.

The goal is—complete immersion.

I can't help a little uneasiness. After all, I don't know what to expect. Will they believe my fake story?

It doesn't take long for two other men to notice the newcomer and to come over to check me out. To my relief, they seem friendly, albeit rough around the edges. They ask me why I'm here, and I tell them I recently split from my wife (not true) and lost my job, all in the same month (also not true, obviously). "Just trying to get back on my feet," I say. "I should be out of here in a month."

They nod, and one of them mutters, "That's what we all said."

If this were reality, my heart would've sunk. But it was enough to elicit a sympathetic nod from me.

Now what? An endless day with nothing to do stretches before me. At least I have my iPad to take notes of my experiences. As the day goes on and I meet more residents, I notice other electronic devices. To my surprise, some of them have smartphones. And several have tablets as well. I want to ask how they're obtained, but I would probably sound like the noob I am.

In a flash of inspiration, I put away my smartphone in my backpack. It's easy to pretend I don't have one, giving me a good reason to chat with my next-door neighbor, a long-bearded fellow about my age, channeling his inner lumberjack in plaid flannel, suspenders keeping a pair of dirty Levis from falling off his protruding belly.

"Hey," I say to Artoo (don't laugh. It's the name he gave me and what everyone calls him.) "How can I get hold of a smartphone like yours?"

He lifts his proudly. "I got this from the guv'ment," he said. "Someone from the city came through here and told us if we wanted a phone, we could have a phone. They made us sign a form, and there you go."

He was apparently referring to the federal program, which provides cell phones to low-income citizens so they can contact emergency services if ever needed and have a way to do their banking.

I soon learned almost everyone in camp has at least one of three things: a bank account in which their disability or social security payments are deposited; a permanent address where all their mail comes (sometimes a post office box for which they pay cash every month; other times they borrow a family member's address); or a smartphone which they pay for via autopay from the aforementioned bank account. Those who don't have a phone likely sold it for drugs at some point in the past. Those on disability who don't have a bank account receive paper checks at their address of choice, which they tote down to the corner check-cashing store. For a three-dollar fee, they can pocket hundreds of dollars in cash to spend as their hearts desire.

I also discovered these folks look out for each other. As in any community, a few bad actors ruin life for everyone else—the ones who steal for drug money, play loud music (they hook their smartphones up to speakers, just like you would), and pick fights. I quickly learned who they were and took pains to avoid them. In this particular camp, there were a couple of young men, in their early twenties or so, high school dropouts, and chronic drug users. Just your everyday no-goodniks (to borrow from my parents' vernacular.) They're the ones who drop through society's cracks, the ones beyond the reach of homeless services. With all the non-profits and government agencies available to help these people, it surprised me so many remain on the street despite the myriad of organizations willing and able to help and the astronomical sums of money thrown at the problem.

But people can't be helped unless two things happen: One, they have to want help getting off the street and into stable housing, and two, they have to know what help is available and have access. It's why non-profit groups and private citizens periodically visit and drop off literature, food, clothing, and other necessities. My favorites are the church groups who come through preaching Jesus and passing out food, clothes, and booklets. They don't realize the residents laugh and mock the "churchies" after they leave, then use those pages as toilet paper. I wish I could tell the God squads how much their efforts are wasted.

Except for this morning. I saw one drug-addicted young man have a come-to-Jesus moment while the "churchies" were here. Apparently, the young addict meant it when he talked about Jesus being Lord, unlike most phonies here who only say it for the free food. To everyone's astonishment, he packed up his tent and left with one of the church guys, yelling to all of us that Jesus had set him free of his addiction, praise the Lord. He invited anyone who wanted to be set free also to come with him. To my amazement, two of his druggie friends followed him out of the camp.

Whew, good riddance, I thought. Three of the most troublesome campers, gone—just like that.

Praise the Lord.

The camp was much quieter after they left.

In a day filled with surprises, the most surprising discovery came at the end of the day. Stay tuned for Part 3 to find out what it was.

Jon sent a quick text. *Great article, Steve.*

Thanks, came Steve's reply. *Already getting backlash. Go read the online comments. Heads up, beware the language.*

Will do. Steve, it's never a waste of time to pass out gospel tracts. We just have to leave the results in God's hands.

Jon set his coffee down and found the article on his phone. Despite Steve's warning, he found himself riveted.

Comments

D.D. – The Mercury - just another leftie rag spouting the same old same old.

J.S. – I lived in Mill Valley until I watched our once vibrant little town besieged by *** aggressive, destructive homeless with no respect for hard-working citizens. I see them urinating in doorways, I see fecal matter in restaurant entrances, theft, vandalism, and dead bodies from overdoses at least once a week on the sidewalk in front of my store. Until SOMEONE in the county steps up and addresses this issue, it will only continue.

P.T. – Agree, the problem is, these aren't actually homeless people, they're mainly *** drug addicts getting free medical and food but won't choose housing or stay in shelters because they want to keep their drugs.... it's sad how we let people get to this point.

D.M. – Hey, why doesn't the county pay the homeless to clean up the camps?

S.S. – So the low-income native Californians displaced by rising rents should go where, exactly?

P.A. – P.T., if you want your state back you need to start by getting rid of ALL the current leadership!!!!

Jon blinked at the string of exclamation marks following P.A.'s comment like a long fence post, at least a hundred of them, enough to cover three cow pastures. He could visualize P.A. sitting at his computer, jaw clenched, steam coming out his nose like an angry bull, blood pressure soaring. Hopefully Mr. P.A. didn't give himself a stroke.

P.T. – A state and a country making the rich richer and the rest of us poorer is what gave us homelessness. Thousands of veterans set adrift after fighting endless, ridiculous wars is what gave us homelessness. Greed gave us homelessness. The rich buying up all available properties for profit, leaving the elderly no place to go but the streets gave us homelessness. The system that throws foster kids into the streets on their eighteenth birthday gave us homelessness. Open your eyes. Go out and hear their stories before you judge what you couldn't begin to understand.

"Isn't Steve doing that?" Jon muttered. He hit reply underneath PT's comment.

J.P. –The writer is doing exactly that. He's sharing their stories with us to help us understand, to help generate a little grace, and not so much judgment.

He had to smile. It sounded like something Meg would say. His soft-hearted wife had rubbed off on him. Wouldn't she be proud.

CHAPTER

Twenty-One

It is only through labor and painful effort, by grim energy and resolute courage, that we move on to better things.

~ Theodore Roosevelt

"Your court-appointed guardian will be here soon to pick you up."

Myla croaked at the pretty nurse, Cheryl. "What court-appointed guardian?"

"Your Uncle Tyler."

Uncle Tyler? She'd added the title in her contacts to allay suspicion, not to assign him an important role. How dare these people snoop through her phone. "What do I need a guardian for?"

Cheryl took Myla's hand in her soft one and gave her fingers a light squeeze. "My dear, you've been very out of it for several days."

Morning sunlight illuminated the room and stung her eyes. Myla wondered if the days had always been so bright. Her stomach no longer teeter-tottered with nausea, and her head had stabilized. Her mouth watered. For the first time in days, she felt like eating.

And getting high. A fresh, shiny Green Goblin would feel so good right now.

She turned to the nurse, who kept speaking. "You probably don't remember, but you tried to leave several times, and we had to restrain you."

"But I'm not a minor. You had no right."

"Oh, but the doctor got a court order to keep you here. Your blood pressure and heart rate were through the roof. You were in extreme danger." The nurse caressed Myla's fingers. "And so was your unborn baby. You're pregnant, you see. We needed to keep you and your baby safe."

Pregnant. It came back to her now. Her last exchange with King-Boy. She felt around for her phone. "How long have I been here?"

"Six days." Cheryl's smile reminded her of the church goers who occasionally visited the homeless camp. "Congratulations. You made it, you little trouper."

She'd survived the worst sickness she'd ever experienced. A gut-wrenching, please-let-me-die horror story.

It was over, but she didn't know whether to rejoice or mourn.

"Can I get my phone now?"

"Sure." Cheryl retrieved it from a cupboard, but it was dead. "Let me go find you a charger. Someone will have one, I'm sure."

After Cheryl brought the charger, Myla stretched out on her hospital bed and picked up her charging phone. No messages awaited. Absolutely nobody had tried to contact her.

Including King-Boy. She allowed a tear to escape since she had no reason to pretend. Nobody here judged her on her cool factor or lack thereof. She could wear her heart on her sleeve all she wanted. Apparently, King-Boy had forgotten the loving words he whispered to her. She scrolled back over the texts they'd exchanged, starting the morning of the sweep and her dopesick episode.

Hey hotsie boi 😌 😌

Beebs 😌 😌

She felt a blush invade her face as she read the next few texts and then skipped to her cry for help.

I need you to come get me. Popo cleared us out.

Where r u?

On Bridgeway. And I got news for u.

Don't make me wait. Tell me now, lil Beebs.

I'm preggo, big Dads.

???

Yep!

Don't call me Dads.

Papa!

**^#(^^##

Back atcha, a##@@

U expect me to believe it's mine, u slut?

She remembered how his words stunned her, like a slap, how her heart nearly stopped. Next thing she knew, she woke up in the hospital, feeling like she'd died and gone to hell.

And now, a blank phone screen. She carried the child of a hard-core playa.

She cupped her belly and whispered. "Don't worry, baby, you'll never have to know what a revolting loser your sperm donor was."

She lay back on the hard hospital mattress, closing her eyes against the radiant morning sun, whispering sweet nothings to her little one in between sniffs. She let her thoughts drift, finally settling on the terrible day she'd ended up here. JJ's death. The sweep. Dopesickness. A frantic search for a fix. After she'd hit a dead end with King-Boy, she'd sent a last resort text to a different number. But only because everyone else had written her off as a lost cause.

"Myla."

The deep voice shook her from her reminiscing. For one delusional, hopeful moment, she thought King-Boy had come to rescue her after all. But then she recalled what Nurse Cheryl had told her…

A familiar spicy scent assaulted her, pulling her back in time kicking and screaming. She no longer wanted to go there.

She opened one eye, then the other. He perched on the edge of the hospital bed, leveling the same cool gray gaze on her, those defined features etched with strength.

"Myla? You awake?"

She opened her eyes to their widest. "Tyler?" So, it was true. Her "uncle" had come to rescue her from this prison. "Someone said you're my guardian."

He crossed his muscular arms over his chest. "One of the nurses here called me after you were admitted. She saw your text and assumed I was your next of kin. Why did you contact *me* for help? It's been months since we've talked."

She croaked out a reply. "I have no place to go."

"And that's my problem … why?"

"Your stepson ghosted me." Pent-up words burst from her. "I want you to know I named our baby Lula. But she died before I even held her."

The look of pity he gave her spoke louder than words. Ironic, considering he'd pressured her for an abortion.

"I'm sorry." Awkward silence thickened between them before he spoke again. "What a hard situation for you."

The nerve of this man. "Of course, it was." She'd turned to Oxy in earnest. Not only from the loss of her precious daughter but from his abandonment.

His eyes softened when he turned to her. Apparently, the message of her trauma finally got through. "I understand you had volunteer sitters twenty-four-seven."

"Really?" She thought she'd dreamed up the strange women at her bedside.

"Yes, the staff was afraid you'd walk out."

"I wanted to, but they kept holding me down."

"They had to call a security guard one time."

"They were a determined bunch, weren't they?"

"They just wanted to keep you and your baby safe."

Her cheeks burned at his frankness. She doubted his stepson had told him of her condition. Which meant the hospital did. Most likely he figured out the baby's paternity also. *Congratulations, Grandpa.*

"Has anyone called to check in on you?"

"Besides the staff and those sitters, nope." She aped his crossed-arm body language. "Not even Debbie or Reuben. Haven't talked to them since the day they kicked me out."

"Maybe if you apologized for stealing from them and worked on paying them back, they'd welcome you back into their lives."

Hmph. They'd refused to let her keep seeing King-Boy. On the other hand, in light of his character revelation, maybe they'd been onto something.

"You were staying with your biological mother for a while. What about her?"

"No. She doesn't want me around either." Tyler didn't need to know Myla had stolen from her, too.

In fact, if she'd had a nurturing, loving mom and dad like other kids had, she wouldn't have ended up on the streets.

Her bio mother had a lot to answer for. Memories pulled at her, threatening to send her someplace she didn't want to go. But, like the pull of Tyler's perfume, she couldn't stop the visions.

That day was imprinted on her mind like an ancient etching, permanent and never changing. She knew the memories would haunt her till the day she died. She'd come home from fifth grade to an empty apartment. Not so unusual. It just meant her mom was out working and would be home later. Myla wasn't too worried. Her mom never told her where she worked or what she did, but it must be something sporadic because her hours changed day by day. She had instructed Myla incessantly: the safest place for her was inside. She warned her not to even go to any of their neighbors' homes because she could get in trouble if they knew.

"Knew what?" *Myla asked.*

"If they knew you were here, alone. We don't know who we can trust."

Myla didn't understand, but she did as her mother instructed. And Mom almost always came home in time for Myla's bedtime.

But not this day. By eight o'clock, when Mom hadn't gotten home, Myla's senses jumped to high alert. Especially when a knock pounded on the door. And no ordinary knock. No friendly-neighbor-coming-to-check-on-you knock. An aggressive, open-this-door-right-now knock. Myla crouched in the narrow space between the sofa and the wall, refusing to answer. Mom's words reprimanded her: "We don't know who we can trust. Some people enjoy talking about other people. We don't want to give them something to talk about, do we?"

Two more knocks, then yelling. "Open up!" Shivering, she crawled to the window. But of course, she couldn't see who stood at the door. Until they turned and left. Two men in cop uniforms stood on the stoop and glanced in her direction, but she darted under the windowsill before they caught a glimpse of her.

What could the cops possibly want? Had the neighbors been talking about them? She crawled into bed, her eyes wide, wishing she were allowed to have friends, or knew someone she could call.

That night they took her away, but not kicking and screaming. She was too frozen with horror to scream or kick. They took her to live with Reuben and Debbie Schwartz, a kind couple, but overwhelmed with four biological kids of their own. The oldest daughter, fourteen, told her her mother had been taken to jail. "What for?" Myla asked.

"Didn't you know your mother was a hooker?"

Later she googled the meaning of hooker and finally understood so much. Her mother's sporadic hours, the strange men she brought home, men who sometimes leered at her. As soon as they did, Mom made them leave. But others she let stay. From the things she'd heard kids at school whisper about, she suspected she knew what her mom and the strange men were doing.

Her mom—a hooker. No wonder her mother always refused to tell her who her father was.

She probably didn't even know.

The memory faded, and she forced her mind back to the here and now. "Have you been here with me the whole time?"

"I stopped in whenever I could to check on you."

His wedding ring glowed on his left hand, shouting the answer to her unspoken question. Which led to another. "How's your son, Tye, these days?"

Deep shadows passed across his face. "He didn't make it."

"Didn't make it? You mean he bit it?"

Tyler winced. "What a crude way to put it. He was found dead last year in Phoenix. They found fentanyl in his system." He stopped and turned, his eyes glittery with emotion. "But you … you have a chance for a better life. You're clean now. Have you any plan at all?"

"Not really." She knotted her fingers around the rough fabric of the hospital blanket. Another awkward silence fell, yet she had so many things she wished to say to him. "Maybe get high again? Otherwise, I think about Lula all the time. It totally sucks."

"After you went through all this, you want more Oxy?"

"It's a painkiller, right? It kills my pain."

"It kills people too if it's not monitored properly by a physician."

"Like it did Tye?"

"Tye refused to listen to me, and now it's too late for him. But it's not too late for you. Ever thought about NA? Narcotics Anonymous? They help you make it through—"

"I know all about them. No thanks."

"Let me see what I can do about finding a place for you." He nodded at Cheryl entering at the same time he left.

"Ready to go home?" she said.

Myla uncrossed her arms and wrung her hands. Surely this nurse knew by now she had no home to go to. "Yyyyep."

"After the doctor signs off on your discharge papers, you're free to go." She handed Myla a brochure. "Here, be sure to hang onto this. You'll need it."

Your Recovery Resources, said the heading. Inside, a list of addresses.

"Find the nearest location to you and follow their regimen religiously," said the nurse, hugging her. "Your life depends on it."

CHAPTER

Twenty-Two

You are hastening toward Eternity, But this body goes slowly toward Perishment. You do not wait for him, And he cannot go quickly. This, my Soul, is sadness.

~ Kahlil Gibran, HAVE MERCY ON ME, MY SOUL

Someone had left a Marin Mercury in the hall, and Myla flipped to the obituary section, half-dreading, half-hoping, what she might find.

A familiar name jumped out at her and grabbed her by the throat.

In Loving Memory ~ Justin James Cooper

Justin Cooper of San Rafael passed away in Sausalito, California, at the age of twenty from an opioid overdose. Known as Just by his friends and family, he was born in Mill Valley and graduated from Golden Gate High School with a 3.9 GPA. A popular student, he was active in many extracurricular activities and sports and was honored to be selected as one of five Salutatorians his senior year. That same year, he played the lead role in the musical *Oklahoma!* He was excited to be admitted to Cal State East Bay as a Music Education major. Tragically, his life ended too soon because of a legal prescription he was given in his first year of college for an injury. The family asks that contributions be made in his memory to the Benson Foundation, a non-profit organization which seeks to educate the public on the dangers of legal opioids, particularly vulnerable youth.

She swallowed around the lump in her throat as she returned to her room to pack up and wait for Tyler. Poor JJ, her best friend for a season. The memory of his cold, stiff body hadn't been a bad dream, but reality. Sniffing, Myla wiped her nose and eyes, then reached inside her left boot in the room's little closet. Her fingers explored till they found what they sought. Shoved to the very end of the toe, her wad of cash.

Now, where'd she stashed the money clip? She needed to hawk it soon. Somewhere, in one of the hidden pockets of her backpack, she'd stowed it away to keep it safe.

She found it in an obscure little pocket, safely zipped. Out of habit, she checked her phone, even though she'd checked it mere moments ago. Hard to believe nobody had texted her. Maybe she needed to check Messenger instead.

Opening the app, she noticed one message waiting. From Connor Paulson, sent several days ago.

Hey Myla, long time no see ... What u up to these days?

She didn't know whether to feel pleased or threatened. Had Connor truly contacted her out of concern, or had Jon recruited his son to check up on her? If he did, it would only mean she *was* the former employee wanted for questioning.

Her finger froze over the message. If she opened it, he'd see she did. And then tell his dad she'd ignored him.

She cleared her throat, her thoughts racing. She needed to get the Paulson family off her trail. Now.

This is Myla's mom, she composed in her head. *Myla passed away.*

Nah. Then word would get around, and she couldn't have her former friends and acquaintances thinking she was dead. What if she needed them someday?

Maybe, *You have the wrong person.*

No. She needed to delete the note without opening it. Let him believe whatever he wished.

Aw, Connor. If only she'd been a better person. *If only I'd deserved a good guy like you.*

She hit delete just as Tyler returned with the news he'd found a place for her.

"Where is it?"

He picked up her pack as she shoved her feet into her boots, wrinkling her toes against the barrier of cash. "It's a women's recovery center in San Rafael. I had to pull some strings to get you to the top of the list." Placing his hand on her back, he sent a firm directive he wasn't giving her a choice. They walked side by side along the corridor. "They'll require you to go through their 90-day program as well as attend NA meetings. If you can manage to stay clean, you'll get to have a roof over your head and three squares a day. They can find you a job, too."

They reached the exit where a security guard examined her paperwork, and then he motioned them through sliding doors out into the hot sunny day. Flawless blue sky draped like a warm sheet above them, and the scent of roses floated from a nearby garden. She breathed deeply, having missed the feel of the great outdoors.

"Will you come see me?"

He gave a noncommittal scoff. "I can't make any promises."

"Of course not."

He didn't flinch at her sarcasm but stopped on the sidewalk and turned. "You can do this, Myla." He placed his free hand on her shoulder. "You're stronger than you think. You'll have a support system in the shelter and at NA to help you through this. You know I can't be all that for you."

Tyler spun and entered the parking garage, shifting her pack to his other shoulder, but never letting go. He knew taking her belongings hostage would force her to go along with his plan.

He knew her well.

A car beeped, and he stopped next to a jet-black Mercedes. She ground to a halt. "Still have Benny, I see." She patted the shiny trunk. "He hasn't changed a bit."

He opened the passenger door for her, then tossed her pack in the back seat. "Unlike you. If I'd passed you on the street, I might not have recognized you."

She settled into the leather seat. "I wouldn't have let you pass me without saying anything."

He nodded. "Yes, I know. That's your problem, Myla." Watching the dashboard display, he backed out. "You've never learned to do life in a responsible way. You're codependent, and you suck people dry."

"Whatever. Can you find out what they did with the dog for me?"

Heard from Connor Paulson today. I could tell he was only trying to find me cuz his dad asked him to. All of a sudden, these memories are flooding me. How sweet he was to me in high school band, how we loved to pound those percussion instruments like maniacs. How he made me laugh so hard, Mr. Barry would give us dirty looks. How pumped he was by my manga art. One of the few people who got it. He was never a jerk like his dad, even though he sure does look like him. If I hadn't been with Max at the time, I probably coulda dated Connor. From the way he looked at me, my gut says yeah, he woulda dated me. How different my life would be today if I'd dumped Max for Connor instead of for Tyler. Connor was the only decent guy who ever showed interest in me. Max was a loser, Tyler a user.

And of course, KB—way-bad-newser. Ha, gotta love that rhyme.

Wonder if Connor has a GF now. Wish I could call him, for old time's sake. Not even an option, unforch, after what I did to his dad. What was I thinking!! No way to go back and undo it. But Connor deserves a good woman. I would've been so bad for him. I would've steered him right off the straight and narrow. Lucky him. He dodged a bullet.

CHAPTER
Twenty-Three

Shoot for the moon; you just might get there!

~ Buzz Aldrin

To: SausalitoJon
From: KevinLipinski

Hi again, Jon,
Sending you some links to several Phleet Powerboats jobs you might be interested in. Let me know if you apply for any of them.
Hoping to be neighbors in the near future!

Kind regards,
Kevin

"Honey," he called.

Meg, holding her morning coffee and massaging her brow, shuffled into the dining room where he sat at his computer.

"I got an email from Kevin." He pointed to the screen. Her hair brushed his cheek as she craned to read. "He sent me some info on job openings at Phleet. Some of them might be a good fit. I thought it couldn't hurt to send a résumé."

Her breathing quickened, and she didn't reply.

"What do you think?"

She clicked her tongue. "I agree it can't hurt, but we really need to bathe this in prayer, my love. If God wants us to move, He'll have to change my heart."

"Ken, thanks for helping me out." Jon wrapped his hands around the paper coffee cup. "The two cops who are supposed to be investigating my case have been slow about following up with me. But I need answers. So that's why I called you."

Ken Tucker sat across from Jon in the corner booth at Sal's, tapping his fingers on the tabletop. "No worries. Give me a quick update on the case. Have the police found any clues?"

"None. The fingerprints on the alarm pad all matched current employees, as I expected."

"No doubt the perps wore gloves."

"I believe Myla Delaney is the most likely suspect and I believe she had help. I'm hoping you can help find her."

"What can you tell me about this Myla Delaney?"

Jon glanced at the handful of clientele sipping drinks or enjoying breakfast, hoping nobody had heard. Ken, the cop, tended to boom when he spoke, but the number of newly empty tables told him the breakfast crowd had started to thin out.

"I just need to know if she's still in the area." Jon broke off a piece of banana bread and kept his voice low, hoping to encourage his wife's son-in-law to follow his example. "Where she's staying, working, et cetera."

"Got it." Ken's tone dropped a few notches. "I'll need her social and her most recent address. First, I'll search the DMV records to see if she has an active driver's license, then look for any current bank accounts under her name."

"I'll get them for you as soon as I get back to the office." For the first time in days, a ray of hope lifted Jon's spirits and encouraged him. Perhaps justice could be wrought. "You should see my shop. The people who ransacked it pretty much wrecked my livelihood. And they need to pay."

A ding from his phone interrupted his words. A text from Connor.

Hey dad, I asked around and nobody knows what happened to Myla. I sent her a message, but she never opened it. Will let u know if I hear anything.

He showed Ken the text. "It's like she's disappeared off the face of the earth. If her own circle of friends doesn't even know where she is, it makes me wonder what she's trying to hide."

"She could be dead."

"I doubt it."

"But if she is, a record of her death will show up somewhere. If so, I'll find it."

Jon leaned in, the edge of the table poking into his chest. "As a police detective, what do you think? Is this what it looks like? Or am I off-base?" As much as he trusted his own judgment, he could use confirmation from an objective third party.

"I think you should trust your gut instincts." Ken drummed his fingers again as though accompanying the syncopation of his thoughts. "Would your alarm monitoring service have a record of activity for the night of the burglary?"

Jon paused, wishing he'd thought of that. "Very good question. It would tell us if someone turned off the alarm after the custodian reset it."

"Yes. Didn't the other cops already ask you?"

"Nope."

Ken shook his head as if amazed at the oversight. "They might have felt it wouldn't prove anything."

"It wouldn't identify the perp, but it would indicate whether it was an inside job."

"I agree. If it were me, I'd call them today."

Back in his office, Jon opened the alarm activity record from the night of the vandalism. His phone pinged with an incoming text.

Carlos's brother, Alejandro.

Alo would have to wait. He turned his attention back to the computer screen.

6:05 p.m. Saturday – alarm set. Patti.

9:37 p.m. Sunday – alarm disabled. The custodians.

10:31 p.m. Sunday – alarm set.

10:32 p.m. Sunday – alarm disabled.

He wrenched his desk chair backward, nearly hitting the wall behind him. Here was proof the perp knew the code.

He scooted closer to the screen and kept reading.

12:55 a.m. Monday – alarm set.

How considerate of them to reset the alarm when they left—after spending over two hours in his shop wreaking havoc. He needed to email this over to Lee and Jackson right away.

Before contacting the police, he opened the awaiting text.

Got a minute?

Jon called Alejandro. "Hey, amigo, what's going on?"

"There's this kid who's been giving me a bad time at the bus stop. He keeps telling me I stink."

"Don't listen to him. He's just being a jerk."

"I want to rub his face in the dirt and make *him* stink."

"My advice to you is the same as my dad used to tell me. Don't use your fists. Use your brain."

"How?"

"Find a way to outsmart him. Make him never want to mess with you again. You're a smart guy. I can tell by the grades you get. I know if you put your mind to it, you'll figure out a way."

Long pause, while his young friend chewed on this. "Gracias, gracias, amigo." The reluctant words told Jon Alo didn't quite believe him yet.

"You can do this. Let me know how it goes."

"Si."

He hung up and checked his email. The top three immediately caught his attention.

> To: SausalitoJon
> From: Phleet Powerboats, Portland OR
>
> Dear Mr. Paulson:
> Thank you for your interest in Phleet. We have received your resume in consideration for the open position of Northwest Regional Director of Marketing and would like to discuss further your background and skills and how they might fit within our organization. If you are interested, please contact our Human Resources department to schedule a video conference.
> Again, thank you for your interest in Phleet Powerboats.
>
> Sincerely yours,
> Kamala Yates
> Vice President of Human Resources
> Phleet Powerboats, Inc.

The second email struck a similar tone. They wanted to interview him for Director of Community Affairs. The third politely declined his application for Manager of Promotions.

At least with a video conference, he wouldn't have to travel out of state.

But what if they offered him a job? Would Meg soften toward the idea of moving? Or harden her resistance even more?

Although he understood her desire to stay here, near her family and everything she knew, he also knew if this was God's leading, Meg would ultimately set aside her desires to follow His will.

He dropped his forehead to his fists and petitioned the Lord. "Father God, you know my desire to start over again in a better place. And you know Meg's desire to stay here. I pray for your guidance, Lord, and I ask we would both proceed according to Your will. If it's Your will for us to relocate, Lord, I ask you would change Meg's heart.

"And if you want us to stay, then change mine."

CHAPTER

Twenty-Four

Is Heaven a physician? They say that He can heal; But medicine posthumous Is unavailable. Is Heaven an exchequer? They speak of what we owe; But that negotiation I'm not a party to.

~Emily Dickinson

In Noelle Marquette's Merchandising Department, Meg checked the time. The morning had crawled along. Ten minutes until lunch break. She needed to put in one more order before she left. Designer shoes scrolled across her screen. Colorful high heels. Flimsy sandals with laces up the calf. Mid-thigh leather boots. None of them for her. Oh, if only she could afford such opulence. The most expensive pair of shoes she owned cost $200 on clearance, but you'd never know it from the simple lines and low heels. She'd paid dearly for the fine leather and Gucci label.

She froze at a pair of $800 pink Versace sneakers. Perfect for a Google or Intel female executive who wanted the jogger look without the actual workout. As she forwarded the link to her boss, Sylvana, for approval, something moved at the corner of her vision. A flash of royal blue materialized into Kassidy, her mouth open.

"Meg!"

"Hey Sid, just in time to see my latest find." Only Meg and Rich were allowed to call Kassidy 'Sid.' "Come look at these Versace shoes. I bet Francine's team could sell a lot of these, right?"

Kassidy allowed a brief glance at the screen, then clutched her middle, her eyes wild, breathing hard. "Richard's been taken to Community Hospital."

Her heart lurching, Meg stood. Her cubicle mate, Julie, tried to hide her curiosity, but her hands hovering over the keyboard, and her flaring nostrils, gave her away.

Her knees weak, Meg anchored herself on the back of her chair. "Holey socks, Kassidy. What happened?"

Her daughter-in-law's voice broke into a sob. "Our next-door neighbor, Jake, found him passed out on the bathroom floor when he came over to play a video game, and called 911, then called me." Sniffing, she wiped the smeared mascara from beneath one eye.

"I have to let Sylvana know. And Jon." Meg fumbled out texts to her boss and husband and, five minutes later, was speeding north on the 101. Her hands white-knuckled the steering wheel as she sped past cars already going seventy. "Was it the Oxy? Did he OD?"

Kassidy held up her wet palms. "I don't know for sure, but that's my guess."

"Did you ever call his doctor's office?"

"No." Kassidy sniffed. "I got busy and put it off."

Meg's lips tightened. "Well, his doctor certainly needs to know about this." Her phone beeped. "Jon will meet us at the ER," she said as they crossed the Golden Gate. Sure enough, he waited for them in the emergency room lobby, then he and Meg checked in with the front desk. The receptionist directed them to have a seat.

"But why is he here?" Kassidy said. Dried tears traced white streaks through the blusher on her cheeks. "What made him pass out?"

"The doctor will be out soon to talk to you."

Five minutes later, a familiar face came through the swinging door. Jon stood to shake Dr. Jenkins's hand. The doctor blinked, then recognition flashed.

"Weren't you two here just last week?" At Jon's nod, he said, "We have to stop meeting like this." His mouth twisted into a wry half-smile, and Meg responded with a feeble chuckle.

"Sorry, bad joke." He grew appropriately somber, then gestured toward the door. "If you two will follow me, I'll take you back to my office."

Meg noticed Kassidy squirming on the chair's hard surface as Dr. Jenkins updated them. "Your son overdosed on OxyContin. We've got him on a drip of naloxone."

"How much did he take?" Her voice wavering, Meg reached for the chair arm but knocked her hand against the edge of the desk. Grimacing, she scooted the chair back and clutched her sore fingers.

"That's not an easy question to answer." The doctor's knuckles whitened as he folded his hands atop the desk. "It would depend on the pills' dosage and how frequently he took them. Good thing your son's a big guy. It easily could've killed a smaller person."

Kassidy's broken sob echoed in Meg's heart. Shuddering, she felt for Jon's reassuring hand. He gave hers a squeeze.

The doctor looked at Kassidy. "How long has he been on Oxy?"

Fisting her hands under her chin, Kassidy ground out, "For several months. He was having bad headaches after he recovered from the shooting last year—"

"The shooting?" The doctor cast her an alert glance.

"Yes, at Ignacio College. Do you remember it? He was one of the injured."

Dr. Jenkins nodded, and his face cleared. "Oh yes, that shooting. So he's been on Oxy ever since?"

"No, he tried some over-the-counter things for a few months, but they weren't helping, so he finally got a prescription."

"Who is his primary physician?"

When Kassidy gave the name, the doctor nodded. "I know him. I assume he's monitoring your husband's usage. Pharmacies won't refill

Oxy prescriptions until only a week's worth of pills remain. It's all tracked in the computer." He keyed something into his laptop. "I'll send these records over to him. He will probably discontinue your husband's opioid regimen and form some sort of solid plan going forward."

A nurse poked her head in. "Doctor, the patient in room 3A is waking."

The doctor rose. "That would be your son. If you don't mind waiting in the lobby, we'll keep you posted on his condition."

Minutes stretched to thirty, then forty-five. Meg tried to read an e-book on her phone, then the magazines and newspapers scattered about. But she couldn't stay seated. She stood up to pace, then found herself at the front desk checking for updates so often, she feared it annoyed the staff. If it did, they hid it well behind pleasant smiles and soft words.

How could Jon sit so calmly? Poor Kassidy had curled up on a couch and fallen asleep. "Pregnant-tired," Meg recalled saying when she carried her two babies years ago. In Kassidy's case, tears exacerbated her weariness.

Jon stayed busy checking emails and sending texts. At one point, he signaled to her he needed to make a phone call, then stepped outside. His animation spiked her curiosity. From his smiles and laughter, she gathered he was getting good news.

What good news could possibly present itself during these dark days? With his business in shambles, his stepson on the brink of death...

Perhaps the cops had found the culprit. Or his insurance agent was offering him a generous settlement. A glimmer of optimism broke through the gloom. They needed something positive right now, something to give hope.

When he returned and plopped beside her, she placed her hand on his arm. "You look pleased, honey. Who was that, and what did they want?"

His face closed up, but he stretched out a lazy smile. "Kevin Lipinski."

It wasn't like Jon to give partial answers. "Oh." She forced a casual tone. "I could tell it was a good conversation. How are they doing?"

"Very well. The kids like their new school. They're plugged into a great church, and Alyssa is enjoying the new neighborhood and making lots of friends."

Why the strained tone? "I'm happy for them."

"Also, they have very little crime in Happy Valley, Oregon." He covered her hand with both of his. "Sweetheart, it sounds like the kind of place we'd enjoy. I got an email from Phleet Powerboats. They want to interview me."

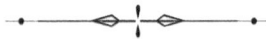

His wife's intent gaze latched onto him. "What did you tell them?"

"I set up a video interview for tomorrow."

"Without discussing it with me first?"

"You were at work, my dear. I thought you agreed it wouldn't hurt to pursue. I'm not obligated to accept a position with them if they offer." But oh, how tempting to say yes. How he itched to leave this place. His business had no future. Crime was out of control, and the politicians who ran the state had no clue how to govern.

He braced himself when Meg asked him, "What would you do with your business?" It wasn't like her to sound so challenging.

"Liquidate everything and walk away." He knew he sounded defensive. He smoothed out his words. "And good riddance to it."

"Don't you have another year on your lease?"

"Yeah, I'd have to find someone to sublease until then. If I can't find one, I'll just have to eat the cost." A deep sigh whistled from deep inside him. "Either way, it's not going to be a piece of cake."

A nurse called their names, snapping the tension like a stretched rubber band. Meg woke Kassidy, and they followed the nurse back to Rich's room, a strained silence throbbing between them.

Meg went to her son's bedside. Richie's eyes were open but sleepy. "He was very tired, so we let him sleep," the nurse told them. "But now he's ready to go home. The doctor wants a quick chat before you go."

After Kassidy signed the paperwork, Dr. Jenkins urged them to get Rich into some sort of treatment plan. "I know of several good ones in the area. He also needs to start going to Narcotics Anonymous meetings." He directed his next words to Kassidy. "And I encourage you to either go with him or start attending Al-Anon meetings. Those are for the family members of addicts."

She nodded, and Meg's heart thumped at the word "addict." Who'd have thought she'd ever hear that word associated with either of her kids.

CHAPTER
Twenty-Five

I many times thought peace had come, When peace was far away; As wrecked men deem they sight the land At centre of the sea, And struggle slacker, but to prove, As hopelessly as I, How many the fictitious shores Before the harbor lie.

– Emily Dickinson

A text from Ken awaited Jon. He rubbed his eyes and retrieved his phone off the nightstand.

Found an active bank account and current driver's license for Myla D. Address? Jon replied.

The Richmond address Ken sent was the same as the shop's record. As Jon recalled, it was her mother's address and had already proved a dead end.

Meg rolled over and lifted her head. "Who is it?"

Jon showed her the note.

"It's a start," she said, propping herself up on her elbow. "At least we know she's still around."

"I need to ask him to check her bank activity to see what branches or ATMs she's using."

"Good plan." She threw off the covers and got up. "I need to hurry. I planned to drive around town before work to see if I can find the girl BB. I'm so afraid she might end up back in a homeless camp."

"Is she already out of the hospital?"

"I don't know. They wouldn't tell me since I didn't have her actual name." His wife shuffled her slippered feet toward the master bath.

"But I did find out the detox process takes a few days, then they're released. The hospital refers patients to services, but it's up to the patients to follow up."

"And a lot of them don't, from what I've heard."

"True." Meg pulled her shoulder-length, honey-colored hair into a scrunchie. He loved to run his hands through its softness. "She's probably been discharged by now," Meg went on, "and I need to make sure she's not back on the street, just for my own peace of mind."

"Is Kassidy going too?"

"No, she doesn't work today."

"You're going by yourself? Not a good idea, honey."

"I don't plan to get out of my car. If I see her, I'll go back later and bring Camille." She rested her hand on the bathroom door jamb. "By the way, speaking of Kassidy, she and Rich plan to start attending NA meetings together." Emotion tightened the skin over her high cheekbones. "I hope and pray it works for him." She turned and enclosed herself in the bathroom, but not before he detected a sheen fill her eyes. Seconds later, the roar of the shower reached him.

His heart hurting for his wife, he thanked Ken, who promised to search for any bank activity from Myla.

A new text buzzed his phone.

Alejandro. *I used my brain instead of my fists like you said. And it worked.* 😊.

Nice! What did you do?

Seconds later, his phone rang.

"Hey, Alo. Tell me what happened."

"I, uh, talked with my younger brother. Carlos. I figured between the two of us we could come up with a plan. We found a can of sardines, and then yesterday morning at the bus stop Carlos distracted Antwan and the other kids with some break-dancing moves. Then Antwan wanted to show us his own moves, so he took off his backpack.

While he was breakin' I slipped a sardine into one of the pockets on his backpack."

"Ah Alo." Jon didn't know whether to scold him or laugh. Revenge, in this case, wasn't sweet, but foul.

"All day at school kids were askin' him what that gross smell was. And all the way home on the bus nobody would sit near him."

"I wonder if he ever found the sardine."

"I dunno, but he never said anything else to me about me stinkin'."

Meg drove slowly along the waterfront. No tent cities, no old vans piled to the ceiling with stuff. She hadn't seen any sign of occupation in the usual locations—beneath freeway overpasses, behind industrial parks, tucked into wooded hillsides. Yet unsightly piles of debris marked the places where they'd camped.

Where could they have gone?

And even if she did find some camps, she didn't plan to leave her car to hunt for BB anyway. Unless BB were in plain sight, Meg had no way to find her.

She sighed at the realization she was wasting her time, headed over to the 101, and prayed all the way to work for God's protection over BB. *God, please keep her safe and sober. And my son, also.*

RECOVERING HOPE, said the calligraphic stencil behind Sister Louise, resident counselor for Casa de Merced Recovery Center. She sat facing Myla at her first one-on-one counseling session. A flock of birds sailed across the blue sky outside the high arched window, beckoning Myla, and she fought a sudden urge to jump up and flee to that blue expanse. If only she could grow wings and fly. If she had a choice, she'd come back as a bird in her next life. A majestic eagle to soar through the clouds, or a beautiful bluebird to elicit admiration. Or a red robin, the harbinger of spring and new life.

What a lovely life—to live as a bird. No addictions. No people to let you down. No …

A throat clearing drew her attention back to the soft-eyed nun looking at her with a raised brow.

"Say again?" She'd been so focused on her fantasy she hadn't heard the sister's question.

"I asked if you've had a chance to review the list of expectations in your admittance packet."

"Yeah."

"Any questions or concerns?"

"Yeah, lots."

"Most of the young women we care for here say something similar. Can you tell me just one of your concerns?"

Myla mentally tracked through the five-page handout she'd only skimmed, then recalled the poster in the front lobby. Twelve Steps to Recovery. "Yeah," she croaked out. "Those twelve steps. They look hard. I don't think I can do them." She watched her fingers twist around each other rather than face the kind nun's possible judgment.

"Have you ever heard the story about the man who ate an elephant?"

Now, what does an elephant have to do with this? She searched the woman's features, wondering if she was joking. "Sounds disgusting."

Sister Louise chuckled. "It does, doesn't it? And how do you think he was able to eat the whole disgusting thing?"

"No clue."

"One bite at a time."

"Hmm."

"You've heard the saying, One Day at A Time?"

Myla nodded. *Who hasn't?*

"All of our Sisters of Mercy Rehabilitation Centers, including this one, emphasize baby steps. You can't succeed at all twelve steps in an instant. So, we take them one at a time, take as long as we need to master each one, before moving on to the next."

Myla's eyes traced the fancy, twining lettering in RECOVERING HOPE as the loops from one letter connected to the next in one long curlicue. She wondered if the artist had adopted the same philosophy. One stroke at a time. One letter at a time. He or she must have visualized the finished work in their head, and then, baby step by baby step, voilà. Done.

For the first time since she entered the hospital, hope nodded at her, infusing her with the possibility that maybe her life could be so much more than she'd ever dreamed.

Another tedious day filled with boring meetings at Casa de Merced. They keep us busy with activities practically twenty-four-seven, most of it dreary, except for free time which is from two to four, every day. Sister Louise isn't bad. But right now I'm watching teev & trying not to think about getting high. It's all we talk about in our workshops, group therapy meetings, individual counseling. The four most overused words ever: Addiction. Drugs. Therapy. Recovery. At least during yoga and fitness classes I get to think about something other than my addiction. I work five hour shifts two days a week at the second-hand shop, doing annoying stuff like displaying grimy merchandise and helping cranky customers find non-existent goods. The only thing I look forward to, besides meals and my sessions with Lou, is art therapy, every day at eleven a.m. I'm the only manga artist here, and the instructor always makes weird comments on my drawings. Stuff like, "BB, the intent expression you drew on that face tells me you are a deep thinker." Or, "Your lines and shapes are so precise. Not everyone can draw such straight lines. What do you think it says about your state of mind?"

It tells me I have a linear mind like a railroad track. A "one-track" mind, ha ha. My mind is always on the same track: how can I get high. But then I remember I have a little fetus inside me, and I remember the video they showed in yesterday's workshop about what happens to drug addicts' babies. Whenever I got high, my baby boy got high too. I'm sorry, little one. (I just know it's a boy.) Your Mommy is a sick addict. But now, because of you, Mommy has good reason to not get high. Higher Power, Help Me.

Unforch, my one-track mind wanders off-track too much. I miss JJ. And Bowie. Even King-Boy. I can't forget the little kid who always cried. Wonder how he'll turn out? Future foster kid?

The tent city wasn't the best living situation I've ever been in, but it was home. And they were my peeps.

CHAPTER

Twenty-Six

In the desert I saw a creature, naked, bestial, Who, squatting upon the ground, Held his heart in his hands, And ate of it. I said, "Is it good, friend?" "It is bitter—bitter," he answered; "But I like it Because it is bitter, And because it is my heart."

~Stephen Crane, IN THE DESERT

THE MARIN MERCURY

THAT HOMELESS LIFE
by Steve Davis

PART 3 OF A 6-PART SERIES

I've been in this miserable tent for two full days—the longest two days and nights of my life. I love camping in the great outdoors. But on the street? I can hardly sleep with all the commotion here. I don't see how anyone can bear the tedium. There's nothing to do here. No jobs, no future, no hope. People spend most of their waking hours smoking various substances, surfing the internet on their phones, or playing internet games. Sometimes a game of Scrabble, or a deck of cards, breaks the monotony.

There are no rules here. To each their own, even if it inconveniences, harms, or disturbs their neighbor.

Would I do this if I weren't getting paid?

Not in a million years.

In Part 2, I promised a big reveal—the biggest surprise of the week. Ready? It's the children. Little kids live here in the camp. Most live with one or two adults, presumably their parents. Toddlers with saggy diapers run around. I see preschoolers with eyes prematurely hardened by life. The oldest child here appears to be around eight. None of them apparently attend school, from what I can tell. Yet school buses drive by here every morning.

All in all, a total of eight innocent children call this place home.

I'll never forget my trip to South America as an idealistic yet naïve twenty-year-old college student. I was completely unprepared for what I saw. The street children in the big cities—hungry little thieves, modern-day versions of Oliver Twist—opened my eyes to a tragic reality and left me forever changed.

But I never imagined I'd see those same third-world conditions here in the US of A.

On my second day in the camp, I took an opportunity to chat with one of the kids. He's a five-year-old named Harlow who lives with his mom and four-year-old sister. In terms of homeless camp standards, you would consider their tent among the nicer ones. I asked him if he was going to start school soon, and he said his mom planned to home-school him. Which leads to the question: how do the homeless teach their kids with no computer, no access to school supplies, and no books? By smartphone?

"I'm new here," I told him. "What's it like to live in a tent?"

"I like camping," he told me. "Mommy makes us hotdogs and hamburgers on her camp stove."

"Sounds good. Do you like camping in the woods better?"

"Yeah. But Mommy likes it here because it's close to the bus and the store."

"Do the noisy cars keep you awake at night?"

He ran a stick along the dirt as he spoke. "No, Mommy makes us sleep behind the … the …" He groped for the right word. "The barry thingy. She hung up a blanket and made a room."

"Barrier?"

"Yeah. But sometimes the dogs bark or people yell and wake me up." Yes, the fighting in the camp can be disturbing. You hear f-bombs and murder threats, screams and insults. It's never quite clear if the persons are intoxicated, high on drugs, or suffering from sleep deprivation. I saw all those and more.

Despite the toxic culture, Harlow was getting his most basic of needs met … food, shelter, and sleep. And, in his innocence, he didn't seem to realize his destitute situation. It reminded me of something my grandmother, who grew up during the Great Depression, once told me. She and her siblings didn't know they were poor because everyone around them was in the same boat.

Harlow and the other kids here don't know any other life. Ultimately, their ignorance could be their salvation.

Comments

M.D. – I am in tears right now. Not only is it shameful that US citizens are forced to live such a life, but children are too. Don't kid yourself that Harlow is happy. He and his sister will NOT grow up unscarred from this experience.

T.M. – Where were all the homeless twenty years ago?

M.D. – I think the city should pay the people in those camps to pick up all the garbage.

C.Z. – I too am appalled. So much for Governor D.'s campaign promises. "Real solutions for our houseless citizens," he assured us. Kick him out of office, and let's get someone who doesn't have their head up where the sun don't shine.

L.M. – STEVE DAVIS for Governor!

P.A. – If you want your state back, you need to start by getting rid of ALL the current leadership!!!!

CHAPTER
Twenty-Seven

I felt a funeral in my brain, And mourners, to and fro, Kept treading, treading, till it seemed The sense was breaking through. And when they all were seated, A service like a drum Kept beating, beating, till I thought My mind was going numb.

~Emily Dickinson

"I'm on my way, sweet daughter of mine." Meg hadn't heard such a level of distress in Linzee's voice since the shooting last year that left Richie in a coma. She'd had to leave work a few minutes early after she got Linzee's call begging her to come over. She had some news. Just *news*, never indicating whether she meant good news or bad. But Meg didn't think Linzee would convey good news with such an angsty squeal.

As she made her way north on the 101, Meg visualized her daughter pacing, with the phone white-knuckled against her ear, staring in fright at nothing, and tried to guess. "Can you give me even a hint?" she'd asked.

"Just come, please. Quick." The word caught on a sob.

Something to do with Ken, probably. Ken had gotten in some sort of trouble in the line of duty. Injured or reprimanded. Or, Meg ruminated, Linzee had been the one to get in trouble at her part-time nannying job. Had one of the parents complained about her performance?

The forty-five-minute drive to Linzee's apartment felt like the longest forty-five minutes she could remember in recent history. But finally, she stood on Linzee's doorstep and rang the bell.

Linzee flung open the door. "Mom!" Worry lines creased her daughter's forehead above eyes shining like a bride's, making a confusing contrast. Her forehead said bad news—her eyes said good.

"I'm dying to hear your news." She pulled Linzee in for an embrace, and Linzee clung to her, hiding her face in Meg's shoulder.

"I'm prggnn."

"You're what?"

"I'm gonna havabbby."

Meg pried her daughter away and clasped her shoulders. "Did you say you're going to have a baby?"

A single nod, her contorted mouth and glowing eyes fighting for supremacy. "And I don't know whether to run screaming or shout for joy."

Meg felt her face split into a wide grin. "Well, I vote for shouts of joy." She pulled her into a tight squeeze. "I can't tell you how excited I am for you. Does Ken know yet?"

"No, I plan to tell him tonight. I just wanted to pick your brain first."

"About what?"

Linzee tugged Meg by the hand into the living room, where they settled onto the black vinyl sofa. The evening sun glowed as bright as Linzee's beautiful blue eyes, burnishing the Ikea shelf in the corner displaying her candle collection. Meg felt that silly-fool grin growing even wider. "What did you want to ask me?"

"I'm scared."

Meg's smile vanished as if a cold wind had swept through. "I was scared too when I was pregnant with you."

"Did you have doubts?"

"Not a one. And aren't you glad? Here you are, twenty-five years later."

"I just keep thinking about what a terrible place this world can be for kids. Drugs and crime are so much worse, Mom, than they were twenty-five years ago. Not to mention the impossible cost of housing around here. I don't want to raise a child in this neighborhood, but I don't see how we'll ever be able to afford a decent house in a decent neighborhood."

Meg thought back to her early days of marriage to Phillippe. "Your father and I were in the same boat for several years. Sure, we struggled, but it was a good struggle, not bad. It took us a while, but eventually, between us, we were able to buy the house on Reno Drive." She reached over to place her hand on Linzee's.

"I know this world can be frightening at times. But you and Ken are going to make amazing parents. You just watch. It really does become intuitive, being a mom. Plus, your little ones will have grandparents who love them very much and will do anything for them. Come here." She pulled Linzee's head to her shoulder. "Jon and I and your dad will be right here for you." *Lord, give me the very words to ease Linzee's fears.*

At once, she knew what Linzee needed to hear. "We're not going anywhere," she said, meaning it.

Richard's first Narcotics Anonymous meeting in a church rec hall wasn't what he expected. He clutched Kassidy's hand. Eight or so people sat in a circle. He squirmed on the hard folding chair, trying to get comfortable. Instead of the down-and-outers with open sores he expected to see, he saw a handful of respectable middle-aged professionals plus a few tired, shabby forty-somethings. Only two attendees he guessed to be about his age, one guy and one woman. Of all of them, the young woman most resembled Richard's idea of an addict. Piercings and tattoos, with rips in the knees of her jeans. Dyed platinum hair with dark roots showing. A sneer, tightly crossed arms. Gave her name as BB. She and Richard were the only newcomers, so Joey, the leader, appointed them to tell their stories first.

Joey, a Native American with a long black braid, started with his history. Alcohol, then drugs. Then crime, and a stint in prison, where he got clean and found the Lord. "I've been clean and sober for nine years. My grown children speak to me now, and my grandkiddos are a big part of what keeps me clean, one day at a time." He gestured at BB. "Your turn, young lady. What brings you here?"

She stared at the floor and spoke with a hard edge in her voice. "It wasn't my choice."

Joey nodded. "That's often the case."

"Casa de Merced made me come here." She went on with a story which started out a lot like Richard's own, with a legal opioid prescription. But at her mention of a stillborn baby, he gave a double take.

He studied Kassidy's belly as if he could stop his unborn child from suffering the same fate. If their baby didn't make it would Kassidy turn to drugs to drown out the grief like BB did? Surely the emotional pain would cut as deep as the constant ache in his head. But his wife shunned all drugs and hopefully always would.

Soon his turn came, and just like that, his tongue froze as numb as it did in sixth grade when he got heckled while giving a book report. He'd long ago forgotten the book's title, but the sensation of wanting to bolt, to drop through the floor, stayed as fresh as if it happened yesterday.

Kassidy squeezed his hand and turned a big, encouraging smile on him. Reminding himself this wasn't middle school, he introduced himself and Kassidy, then stumbled through his story—the shooting that made national news, the coma, the long months of recovery.

The migraines.

"Oxy was the only thing to make the headaches go away," he told the group, refusing to look at anyone straight on lest his mind go blank again. These people were strangers, and even though Joey had assured everyone "what's shared here stays here," nonetheless, they all remembered his story, judging by the nods of recognition. He wasn't comfortable in the limelight. "But eventually, I ended up passed out on the bathroom floor. So now I go to the clinic every day for my shot of Suboxone. I hope one day I won't need it anymore."

"How are your headaches?" someone asked.

"My doctor prescribed me a migraine medication, and so far, it seems to be working."

BB regarded him for several seconds, and he looked away, wondering what she was thinking.

Myla remembered that dude from the news last year. The good-looking football player, as she'd thought of him then. But now, with his gaunt frame and sunken cheekbones, she wouldn't recognize him on the street.

Hadn't Jon Paulson mentioned a connection to one of the victims? She couldn't remember who … she'd never really paid attention whenever Jon droned to Patti about his humdrum personal life. She needed to ask this dude if he knew Jon.

On second thought, no way. For a moment, she forgot she was undercover.

The dude's wife kept watching her. *Don't worry, girlie, I'm not after your husband.*

Could she trust these strangers with her newly discovered secret? They'd probably seen and heard everything and were no longer shocked by anything.

"Myla, did you have something to add?" She'd raised her hand without realizing it. She nodded to Joey, and then sought out the kindest face in the room—a forty-something African American grandma type in a bright-fuchsia shawl—and directed her next statement to her.

"Um, I wanted to add ... I ... I'm pregnant."

CHAPTER

Twenty-Eight

Adrift! A little boat adrift! And night is coming down! Will no one guide a little boat Unto the nearest town?

–Emily Dickinson

The grandma woman clucked at Myla in sympathy. "Getting clean was the best thing you could've done for your baby," she said.

Myla nodded, scanning the circle for any judgment. Nothing. These people had been everywhere, heard everything. For the first time since she got here, she realized she was with her kind of people. Too damaged and broken to ever point fingers at you, yet slowly healing.

People she'd known who'd been through substance abuse recovery, she mused, possessed certain qualities others lacked—a healthy awareness of their own fallibility, a take-life-as-it-comes attitude. An approachability that made her feel safe. They didn't put on airs like those who'd never known the sordid side of life.

Perhaps soon she'd become one of them.

Joey's words caught her like a web. "When the meeting is over," he told them, "we'll all leave together. Drug dealers like to hang outside NA meetings."

She visualized King-Boy in his cool car waiting for her outside. Memories assaulted her, recollections of traveling from drug store to drug store, buying stashes of OxyContin for him with fake prescriptions. He always gave her a cut of the profits and plenty of

Green Goblins. The image of those little green pills made her mouth water, and her insides crawled, remembering the sweet high.

"Did anyone not drive here?"

Myla raised her suddenly shaky hand. Sweat broke out on her brow. She needed Oxy like her next breath.

"BB? Are you alright?"

She shook her head and managed, "Wondering if my baby daddy is out there with some Oxy."

Recognizing the signs of impending doom, they all surrounded her, laying hands on her and reciting mantras.

"Let go and let God. You are worth it."

"This too shall pass, lovely lady."

"Visualize a beautiful life of sobriety."

Gradually her heartbeat relaxed, the craving loosened, and she raised her head. "Thanks." Her voice, a mere croak, had yet to catch up.

On the way out, Joey and Grandma Char, her new friend, flanked her. Joey gestured to a far corner of the parking lot. "There's a dealer now. He won't get out, though, if he sees us bunched up. Safety in numbers."

Since Myla'd taken the bus, Char drove her back to the center and made sure she got inside and checked in.

If not for her new NA friends, she'd probably be getting high right now. "Thank you, Higher Power, whoever you are," she whispered once in her room. "Thanks for running interference for me."

"How was the NA meeting?" Meg glanced sideways at Kassidy in the front seat of her Mustang.

Kassidy stared out the window at the orange spires of the Golden Gate Bridge. "I think it's going to be helpful. After Rich warmed up,

I think he really enjoyed it. We met another preggie lady, and she's about my age. We chatted afterward, and she told me she's about three months along. The dad is out of the picture."

"Poor girl. It's so difficult for a woman to raise a child without the other parent around."

"She's in rehab and is worried she'll relapse once she gets out." Kassidy sighed. "I hope she can find a safe place to live."

"We could ask Candy to take her in."

"Candy? Your cray-cray friend?"

"Candy is not crazy. In fact, she's doing amazingly well since her breakdown last year. She's come to terms with her grief over her son, finally, and she's doing for other young women what someone did for her when she was a pregnant high school dropout."

"Which was …"

"Provided her shelter until her baby was born."

"Candy's doing that now?"

"I haven't talked to her for a while, but last time we talked, she was. She's got plenty of room in her big house out in Lagunitas, and her walk with God is solid. She feels it's what the Lord wants her to do."

Kassidy demonstrated her skepticism by pursing her lips and scrunching her brow, which only spurred Meg on.

"She's legit, Sid. She's been licensed by the state as a halfway house manager with the non-profit Our House. One young woman is living there now, but Candy has room for at least two more. Will you talk to your friend at the next meeting? It would put my mind at ease."

"Well, all right."

"And I'll ask Candy if she's willing to shelter her for a while. As long as the woman understands she is required to stay clean and sober…What did you say her name is?"

"She called herself BB. But—"

"BB?" At the name, Meg's brows lifted. "I wonder if she's the same BB I know. What does she look like?"

After Kassidy described her, Meg nodded. "She must be the same BB Camille and I were with when she collapsed. I've been worried about her."

"Really? What a coincidence."

"I don't believe it's a coincidence. I think it's the hand of God moving. I've been praying to find her and make sure she's okay. And safe. I'll talk to Candy today."

Twenty-Nine

The rat is the concisest tenant. He pays no rent ... Hate cannot harm A foe so reticent.

~Emily Dickinson, THE RAT

THE MARIN MERCURY

THAT HOMELESS LIFE
by Steve Davis

PART 4 OF A 6-PART SERIES

The piles of garbage here remind me of scenes from my trip to South America. In third-world countries, basic services such as garbage pickup go unmet. But here in California, the world's fifth-largest economy? For most of us, we pay a company to pick up our trash. But not here in Camp Homeless. Nobody picks up trash here, so the residents toss it wherever. No wonder the stench permeates this place. You need to be very careful where you step, lest you puncture your foot on broken glass or, worse, used hypodermic needles.

I can understand why over 75 percent of my fellow tent-dwellers use drugs (I say this with reluctance). Who wouldn't want to escape this reality? If I were truly living here and not on assignment, I'd be tempted to drown myself in booze or heroin, too.

Where do they get their heroin and other drugs, you may wonder. And how do they pay for them?

I'll answer the second question first. They get their drug money from generous donors like you. All they need is a cardboard sign and a few bleeding hearts, and voilà, they have their next fix. Or their next pack of cigarettes and bottle of wine. A pawn shop half a mile east will hock their stolen goods. They have all sorts of creative ways to come up with a desperate fast buck.

With clearance from my boss, I decided to give panhandling a try and see what it's like to beg for money. I soon found it required a dramatic adjustment in body language—drooping head and slumped shoulders. Deliberately mussed hair. My bushy beard completed the package, and off I went to the nearby corner. Before I went, however, two of my experienced compadres filled me in with some surprising details. One of them, Wheels, told me he'd once made three hundred in one day. "What'd you spend it on?" I asked him. "A brand-new tent," he drawled, "and two liters of Knob Creek bourbon. But last month, I only averaged twenty-five dollars a day. Pays for my booze and a decent meal since food stamps don't stretch far enough." Wheels is from Kentucky and moved out here ten years ago for the sunny weather. But alcohol addiction and divorce took their toll on his job and finances, and he's been on the streets ever since.

My other companion stands on the opposite corner. He's a bit more upbeat at the prospect of today's take. "My mom told me this is America," he said with a grin, "and I could be whatever I want to be. Well, I want to be a panhandler." When I asked him how he arrived at his profession of choice, he said, "Why break your back at a job you hate when you can make as much or more like this?"

He's got a point.

I buy a marker from the convenience store, scrounge up some cardboard (not a difficult task in a dump), and scrawl, HUNGRY

AND HOMELESS, ANYTHING HELPS, GOD BLESS. Five minutes after I get to my corner, a guy in a Mercedes opens his window and hands me a five-spot. I wave thanks and wait some more. A lady in a Toyota drives by, and her passenger opens the window and shouts at me, "Get a job, loser!" (Ha, the joke's on her. I stifle the feelings of shame by telling myself she doesn't know I'm doing my job.)

Most people avert their eyes when I try to make eye contact. I feel invisible, ignored. But some show a measure of compassion. One lady hands me a twenty. Another hands me a store-bought packaged sandwich. Several people curse at me and call me names. But by noon, I have a total of seventy-three dollars and fifty cents in cold, hard cash, a roast-beef sandwich, a bag of corn chips, packaged cookies, three bottles of water, and two gospel tracts informing me I can be sure I'm going to heaven. Sounds like interesting bedtime reading.

I call it a day, knowing now how it feels to make a living at this. I do not envy those who do this day after day. It must chip away at their self-respect, their sense of dignity, and their self-worth. Note to readers: Do not, under any circumstances, major in Panhandling 101 unless you don't mind verbal abuse, name-calling, and demoralizing stares.

Now, back to my first question: Where do the tent-dwellers get their drugs? The answer is: Pharmer Boy, the alias I use to refer to the camp's drug dealer, whose real handle will remain confidential for the purposes of this article.

I was surprised the first time I saw the infamous Pharmer Boy. The way my neighbors talked about him, I expected someone bigger, tougher. But he's practically a kid. Late teens, I'd guess. Maybe early twenties. Long brown hair, olive skin, expensive leather jacket. When he first drove up in his red, late-model sportscar on my second day, I tried to get a photo of him in case my editor might publish it. But my neighbor saw me lift my phone and warned me not to. I should have listened. Pharmer turned and saw me with my phone lifted, ran my way, and before I knew what he was doing, he shouted a curse at me, then launched a roundhouse kick at my phone. It flew from my hand and would certainly have been ruined if it had landed on a hard surface. Instead, lucky for me, it landed in the grass. "Put your *** phone away, ***," he yelled. I got the memo. No photos of the drug dealer. No way for my readers to identify him.

I watched him as he made his rounds. He stuck his head into several tents, then sat on the grass as his customers gathered around. He must have collected hundreds of dollars in cold cash during the short time he stayed, handing out baggies. I estimated about 70 percent of the individuals who call this place home bought meth, heroin, or Oxy from him. They've been at it a long time. You can see it in their drug-worn, leathery faces, even in the younger ones.

People like Pharmer Boy make the world a sorrier place, destroying lives for mega cash. And why not? In a climate where you can earn ten times as much for an hour of selling drugs than you would in a day's work at your local McDonald's, where the war on drugs has been all but abandoned, incentives to change vanish. Cops respond only if someone's life is at stake. Or if they've been ordered to do a sweep. (I hate that word. As though humans can be tossed into a dustpan by some cosmic broom.) The buying and selling of illegal drugs are virtually ignored by local law enforcement.

But I have a plan. For privacy's sake, I can't tell you what it is. It will have to wait for a later issue. Stay tuned.

Comments

P.A. –You have an obligation to reveal this drug dealer's real name. Trust me, we will take care of him.

T.P. – You again, P.A.? Is that a threat, P.A.? How about you tell us YOUR real name, so we can have you arrested for being a menace to society?

P.A. – T.P., you're hilarious. While the real menaces to society walk free, you'd rather target the hard-working, law-abiding citizens who are trying to PROMOTE safety and protect YOUR kids and YOUR neighborhood.

M.E. – Steve Davis, thank you for this series and for being willing to go into the trenches to give us an eyewitness account of this very serious crisis. Even though it wasn't a pleasant experience, we needed to see through your eyes and hear with your ears what is really going on. PS – I assume you will be offering practical solutions and tips for effectively communicating our concerns with our elected officials?

J.B. – With the taxes we pay here in Marin County and California, you'd think we could afford more mental health facilities and shelters. The homeless are multiplying faster than we can build. Why are they reproducing faster than the general population? Oh, wait. Those aren't offspring. They're out-of-staters. Which leads to the question … why are so many of them coming here, and who's taxing them? Oh, my bad. NOBODY!!

CHAPTER
Thirty

There is no deeper desire Than the desire to be revealed.

~Kahlil Gibran

Myla waited until the morning after the NA meeting to satisfy her curiosity about her fellow addict, Richard. Odds were small he was the victim Jon Paulson mentioned. But you never know.

Ignacio College shooting, she googled as she sat cross-legged on her bed, waiting for one of the bathroom showers to vacate. No surprise when a facility had just two showers to be shared among ten women.

The screen filled with links. FOUR DEAD, TWO CRITICALLY INJURED IN LATEST SCHOOL SHOOTING, read the top headline, followed by the photo she remembered—Richard in a football helmet. Richard St. John said the caption. So, not a Paulson. She clicked his name to see his bio. "Richard St. John, aged eighteen, was a freshman at Ignacio. He is the son of Meg Paulson of San Rafael and Phillippe St. John of Santa Clara." Meg Paulson? Jon's wife? She tried to remember the few months during her employment at Paulson's shop, whether his wife ever visited. She drew a blank and returned to the article. "He hoped to collect and restore classic autos someday. During his senior year at Peninsula Christian Academy, he was the star offensive tackle for the Crusaders. On the day this issue went to print, he was in a coma at Marin General Hospital, his prognosis unknown."

In the process of searching, she happened upon a headline about an incident from a few years back, a hot news item she vaguely remembered. WOMAN MISSING FOR FOUR DAYS FOUND SAFE. "Linzee St. John, reported missing last Wednesday, was found confined in a basement in a San Rafael house. The home's owner was arrested …" She skimmed down the article for any familiar names, landing on one. "Linzee's mother, Meg St. John, credits God for the rescue but also mentioned several friends who helped her search. 'Linzee's roommate, Nena Vasquez, played a huge role. She's the one who figured out who had taken Linzee. And I want to mention two other friends, Jon Paulson and Camille Patterson, who were there for me on my grueling journey."

Jon and his wife were newlyweds. From what she'd just read, these people had had more than their share of hard times. And thanks to her, Myla Delaney, life had piled on even more.

She wondered if she'd ever forgive herself for letting King-Boy talk her into that dang break-in. Not for the first time, she wondered why he'd been so insistent. When she'd quizzed him, he offered a vague "making The Man pay." "Don't you want to make him pay for firing you?" he'd said.

The one who needed to pay was King-Boy for dumping her. In a way, he'd done the same thing to her Jon did. And when she got out of here, she'd make sure he paid.

"We talked about Step 8 in group today," Myla told Sister Louise. Today, no birds cut across the slate-gray clouds on the other side of the window. The phrase on the wall buoyed her foolish dream of the good life—RECOVERING HOPE—and promised the very thing she thought she'd never attain: a healthy future. The kind of future other people got to have, not her. But why not her? Why not get a life with houses and picket fences, food in the cupboards, and babies galore? Didn't she deserve hope like everyone else? She mentally glommed onto the words as she met the sister's razor-keen gaze. "You know, Step 8 is the one where we have to make a list of people we've harmed and be willing to make amends."

"I can tell by your expression that doesn't sit well with you."

"My list is gonna be ten miles long."

"You'd be surprised how many clients say the same thing."

"You know, Sister Louise, no matter what I say, you tell me others have already said it. Is there nothing unique about my life experience?" She didn't mean to come off so challenging, and fortunately, the good Sister Louise didn't flinch.

"I know it feels like you're not unique, but that's just because most addicts have so many life experiences in common. And a lot of the same hurts. I bet you've found yourself connecting with some of the other ladies, haven't you? You've found you relate better to them than to most other people you know?"

"You're right, I have. I've bonded with a few, like my sponsor Roberta, but it seems like most of the ladies I've connected with are finishing the program and will soon leave."

"I'm glad you're working with Roberta. She's solid. Now, back to your worries about the steps. Which steps have you mastered so far?"

"Still working on Step 3, turning my life and will over to God."

"And how is that working out for you?"

"I've been reading the Bible and the other church literature they gave me. Trying to pray. The first steps were straightforward, much less difficult than I expected. I mean, it was super easy to admit my life was out of control. It isn't going to be hard at all to do a searching moral inventory of myself. I did it all the time when I lived in the tent, kicking myself over and over for all my shortcomings. But I'm afraid I'll get stuck on steps 8 and 9. How can you guys expect me to go back to all the people I've stolen from and lied to and make amends? Are you serious? They hate me!"

Louise stayed quiet and let her rant until Myla finally flew up her hands and slapped them down on her thighs.

"Myla, you don't have to worry about those steps today. Remember what Jesus said about each day having enough trouble of its own and not to worry about tomorrow? He was completely on board with the one-day-at-a-time philosophy."

"Yes, but that day will come eventually. What's the old saying about paying the piper? I'm completely unprepared to show my face to my foster parents, my mom, my former boss, the homeless guys I filched cash from sometimes—"

"You were in pain."

"Of course, I was."

"Take it to God, Myla. Take your burdens to Jesus."

"Easy for you to say. You've never lost a baby or been rejected by the man you love. Is that why you became a nun? You wanted to be spared the tragedies of life?"

The nun's normally kind face edged with a sternness Myla hadn't seen. "This is not about me, Myla. This is about you. Tell me about your baby. And the man you loved."

Myla told her, the story running as freely and out of control as though someone had busted a dam wide open.

When she'd spent herself, all she had left were sobs, as dark and deep as the ocean.

A box of tissues somehow landed on her lap, and she pulled out a clump in gratitude and swept them across her tear-cleansed cheeks.

"Myla, look at me."

She dared a peep upward.

"I think those tears have been long overdue."

Myla nodded, unable to speak.

"And now I have some homework for you."

Another nod.

"Read one Psalm every day so you can get to know God."

"It sounds too easy."

"It is easy. As you read, you'll learn that God is a redeeming God."

"What do you mean?"

"I mean, He makes things new. He can take bad people and make them good. He can take tragedy and bring good out of it."

"How can He bring good from a dead baby?"

"Why don't you ask Him?"

Myla rubbed the knee poking through the hole in her jeans. Still so much about religion and God she didn't understand. "What if He doesn't answer?"

"He promises He will answer those who seek Him with all their hearts. Someday you will look back and see the hand of God all over your life. I promise."

CHAPTER
Thirty-One

There is always satisfaction in the reflection that, if there were no trials, there would be no victories.

~Anne Sullivan

With Meg's concerns over BB's future settled, she breathed easier. Kassidy promised to accompany Candy to the shelter to meet BB and offer her a place to live after her ninety days. Fortunately, the young woman currently under Candy's roof had stayed at the same shelter and could vouch for Candy. Meg again turned her focus to her family's crises—her husband's struggling business, his desire to flee California, and her son's one-day-at-a-time sobriety. But also, the joyful anticipation of another grandchild on the way.

Ken had texted Jon this morning, which he shared with Meg. *I didn't find any trace of ATM activity for Myla in past two weeks,* Ken wrote. *3 weeks ago, she used an ATM three times at a 7-11 on Harbor Dr a few blocks from your shop. Same week her bank account shows two auto deposits from State of CA for $108 each, several debit card transactions at 7-11 and Ooh La Latte coffee shop. Hope this helps.*

"Yeah, it does," Jon muttered. "Proves she was in the vicinity of my shop."

"And not just passing through," Meg observed. "Sounds like she spent several days in the area. I wonder what she was doing and where she was living."

At her husband's side, Meg watched as he replied to her son-in-law. *Find out if she rented a place nearby. Doable?*

Yep, came the reply.

"But if she's couch-surfing," Jon said, "she'll stay under the radar. It wouldn't surprise me if she hung out at the homeless camp."

"I'm curious to know why she hasn't used her debit card for two weeks."

"She wouldn't need to if she 'took the money and ran.'" He lifted his phone and typed his reply. *Keep looking!*

Myla sat with one palm cradling her belly, even though it barely pooched out at this early stage, and with the other, shook the hand of the woman beside Kassidy.

"Hey," yelled Adelle, the ogress at the front desk. "No touching. Stay six feet apart."

Myla snatched her hand back, having forgotten the ridiculous rules for a moment. Visitors to the shelter were carefully screened for drugs or other contraband. She'd heard Adelle make Kassidy and her friend leave their bags at the counter and tell them to meet BB in the common room. Thank goodness Adelle used Myla's nickname, not her actual name. She couldn't reveal her real name to anyone, knowing Jon Paulson had most likely given her name to the police. No telling if the media had revealed the prime suspect's name in connection with the vandalism by now. She hadn't seen a newspaper for days, and she'd seen nothing on the local news broadcasts yet. What if her photo was circulating in the media?

But then she recalled her transformation from a long-haired, plump brunette to her current incarnation of skinny platinum blonde. She probably worried for nothing.

Five-ten, two-hundred-pound Adelle watched their every move from her perch, just in case her two visitors decided to slip her a forbidden pill. Or cigarette.

As if.

Kassidy introduced her friend as Candy Burton. A name evoking images of her favorite game app, Candy Crush. She wouldn't have any trouble remembering it. She even looked like a Candy—small-boned and thin in her colorful peasant dress and fine wind-swept hair. In fact, because of a startling resemblance between her and Kassidy, they could pass for sisters.

Candy craned to look at her, hands folded in her lap. "BB, I just wanted to meet you since I heard you might need a place to live after you leave here." Her delicate hand swept the room, where two other residents lounged in their PJs watching a rerun of *Friends*. To pass the time, you had a choice of TV or books. No phones or internet allowed here. Messages were left at the front desk, and telephone calls could be returned on the community phone on the side wall. She supposed, grudgingly, she could see the reason for it. Anything distracting them from getting totally clean had to go. But it sure sucked.

"You have a place for me?"

"I do. Another young lady about your age is staying with me, and she got clean here too. Her name is Kimby. Sweet girl. I think you'd like her."

Myla wasn't so sure. So far, she hadn't met anyone "sweet" whose personality wasn't as overripe as a brown banana, like the old Myla. But she nodded. "Sure."

"I know you were on the streets for a while." Her voice was as soft as you'd expect it to be from her appearance. "So was Kimby. And so was I—a long time ago. If someone hadn't taken me in, I don't think I'd be here today."

"I'm three months pregnant."

"So was I."

"Really? How far along were you when you got clean?"

Candy's gaze fell to her twining fingers. "I never really got clean. Used drugs off and on the entire nine months." When she looked up, Myla caught her breath at the gleam of moisture in the other woman's eyes—deep, sad craters. She started to reach for Myla's knee, then pulled her hand away as if she'd suddenly remembered the rules. "My baby was born addicted to drugs. He screamed for his first twenty-four hours. When he grew up, he suffered from terrible mental disorders, and I don't want to see such a fate happen to anyone else. I want to do whatever it takes to keep other young women from enduring what I did."

Myla stifled a shudder. Lucky for her unborn baby, she'd gotten clean before she damaged him or her. At least, she hoped.

She needed to talk about something less painful. She searched her mind for a random, innocuous question.

"How do you two know each other?"

Kassidy settled on the stiff armchair to Myla's right and Candy on the other. "She's a friend of Meg's, my mother-in-law. Meg is the lady who called the ambulance for you."

"Oh, her. The sandwich lady." Meg.

Meg? Richard's mother?

Candy tilted her head. "Sandwich lady?"

"Yeah, she and her friend brought sandwiches to the campsite a couple of times."

She recalled the kind lady and her hard-core extrovert friend, the redhead, had given her a peanut butter and jelly sandwich. In her hunger, it was the best-tasting sandwich she'd had in a long time. Afterward, the Sandwich Ladies had headed in the general direction of the Paulson shop. She hadn't thought anything about it at the time.

Of course. She was Jon Paulson's wife.

"What is Meg's last name?" she blurted before she could stop herself.

"It's Paulson. Why do you ask?"

Myla shrugged to cover the jolting of her heart. "Just thought she looked familiar."

Candy kept talking, but Myla only heard snatches through the roaring in her head. How could she possibly live with this lady who was apparently a good friend of the Paulsons?

But where else could she go?

Candy was saying something about a shooting. And Kassidy's husband.

"I met Meg when she and I attended a grief group after the shooting last year. Her son had been injured, and an old friend of mine from high school was one of the fatalities. We bonded over our shared grief."

"Yeah, he told us his story at the NA meeting."

The roaring subsided and then flared to life again. Candy said her name, forcing her back to the moment. "BB, were you living in the area at the time?"

Myla nodded, unable to speak, her brain still reeling.

"Did you know anyone who was affected by it?"

She shook her head, heart shuddering. She'd have to tell this nice lady she couldn't live with her. But what excuse could she give?

"Time's up," Adelle called. Or rather, yelled, like she knew Myla couldn't wait for her visitors to leave.

Candy blinked. "We're done," she said over her shoulder, then she and Kassidy stood. Facing Myla, she said, "Real quick, before we go, is BB short for something? Like Brianna? Brittany?"

"You look like a Brenna," offered Kassidy.

Myla shrugged as she stood, itching for them to leave. "It stands for Betty Boop. My Grandma's name for me."

Mercifully, the two women said their goodbyes, promising to return next week. *Please don't.* Myla turned her attention to the episode of *Friends* to distract herself from the shock of the sandwich lady's identity.

She took out her phone and opened her journal.

> Mind blown. Sandwich lady is JP's wifey!!! Wonder what Candy and Kassidy would think of me if they knew what I did. Not so anxious to provide me a roof now, are you, Candy Cane?

She'd have to find a different NA meeting now.

She still had no place to go when she got out of here in three months. She couldn't go back on the streets. The addiction would seize her again if she did, and she couldn't shake the horrifying story of Candy's baby and the agony of withdrawals in a newborn. She cradled her belly protectively. This baby could never replace Lula, but maybe he or she would replace the grief with joy. She vowed she'd never ruin this baby's life like Candy did hers.

She had to stay clean.

And had to stay out of prison.

Whatever it took.

CHAPTER
Thirty-Two

A door just opened on a street—I lost, was passing by—And instant's
width of warmth disclosed, And wealth, and company.

~Emily Dickinson

Jon opened his office computer and forced himself to click QuickBooks. Time to stop burying his head in the sand and confront reality. Which meant facing evidence that his business, after ten successful years, wasn't going to make it another year. Dwindling revenue plus skyrocketing taxes plus no new clients equaled failure.

The shop was quiet today. His last new project had come in the Friday before the break-in, and since then, word of his misfortune had spread like a malevolent virus. Many of his regular customers, even potential ones, had decided to take their business to two of Jon's competitors in the city, even though they were further away and far more expensive. The absence of vessels on the shop floor was a new, unwelcome sensation. The insurance company had hauled away all but three boats to get parted out and then paid out most of the final settlement to Jon's customers. The remaining boats, less damaged, would take his crew many more days of work to repair. He couldn't charge his customers for the extra labor and materials. Thus, he faced a severe loss of revenue. Not to mention his paltry portion of the insurance settlement.

Today, the lack of commerce echoed its silence around the vast space, broken up by the occasional hum of the sander as Mark strove to save the lesser-damaged boats. Confident they could be restored as good as new, Fred and Mark had stayed well into the evenings the past week. They deserved a generous bonus before Jon had to let them go and shut down the operation.

One more regretful review of the email from Kamala Yates at Phleet, full of accolades over the second interview yesterday, only emphasized his new normal. He'd made the cut for the final two candidates for Northwest Regional Director, and she wanted to fly him up to Portland for an in-person interview. This morning, he and Meg prayed together after he showed her the email. They prayed for God's clear direction, and they prayed for peace. Yet he couldn't stop a fleeting request—*God, please say yes*—from crossing his mind.

After the prayer, Meg had leveled with him. "Jon, I don't feel any peace about relocating. I'm still so worried about Rich. What if he relapses? What if Linzee needs my help with the baby? I'm sorry, my love." She'd wrapped her arms around his shoulders and looked him square in the face. "I know how much you're worried about our future, but I hope you'll consider my feelings. I know God will provide. Maybe He'll lead you to something locally."

"Of course, Sweetheart," he'd murmured, her words banishing the excitement snaking up his spine after he'd read the email. "But I wonder if Ken and Linzee would be interested in moving to Oregon too."

"I can run it by them." But doubt filled her words.

"On second thought, I can't see them wanting the added stress of a move while expecting a baby." Just like that, his horizon darkened again. He managed to add, "We're a team. I don't want to do anything if you're not a hundred percent on board." He squelched a sigh. "I'll reply today and decline the offer."

He loved Meg too much to coerce her out of her comfort zone. And now, with his dream dashed, he adjusted his keyboard, sent a silent prayer heavenward, and began to type.

THE MARIN MERCURY

THAT HOMELESS LIFE
by Steve Davis

PART 5 OF A 6-PART SERIES

You can lead a horse to water, as they say. But you can't make it drink.

You can open homeless shelters and build affordable housing, but you can't make them go.

Many of you probably believe if we just had enough affordable housing or opened more homeless shelters, we could get those people off the street. After a week in a homeless camp, I can assure you this is not the case.

In a week full of surprises, the shattering of this common belief sits near the top. *But Steve,* I hear you thinking. *Why would anyone willingly live in such horrid conditions if they had other options?*

When you live in a drugged stupor 24/7, you don't notice your surroundings. The high inside feels so good—nothing else matters.

I told you in the last article I had a plan. It involved a bike, several changes of clothes, and a backpack. All these I obtained early on the fifth morning from my wife, with clearance from my boss to whom I confessed my scheme, based solely on a strong hunch. He set me free to follow my gut after some heavy persuasive powers on my part (thanks, Ray!).

Part One of my plan: stuff three completely different T-shirts in my backpack. One was solid green, one was a California Bears jersey, and the last one was a white Yosemite souvenir tee. Next, I stashed two bike helmets: one in gold-speckled black and one in pure white.

I then donned a plain white tee, a pair of inconspicuous dark blue gym shorts, dirty gray sneakers, and wire-rimmed sunglasses, stuffing a second, black-rimmed pair of shades in my pack.

The bike was a common one around here which shouldn't attract attention: a black 2015 Cannondale. I wheeled the bike into my tent and waited. About two hours later, Pharmer Boy arrived. He always took about an hour to service all his clients. In the meantime, I wheeled the bike toward the street where his snazzy ride waited and rested next to a strip mall offering a clear view of his car. I'd be able to see him, but he probably wouldn't notice me.

For the first time, I noticed a young lady in the passenger seat scrutinizing her phone. Soon Pharmer strode to his car and got in the driver's seat. The young woman barely spared him a glance as he merged into traffic, and I rode to the sidewalk. His car proved easy to follow.

As I tailed him, doubts ensued. He could be merely going home. Maybe he was taking the young woman home. Or, and this was what I hoped for, he might be dropping off "merchandise" to more customers. At each stop, I planned to change my shirt and helmet, banking on the likelihood that, if he noticed me, I'd pass for an anonymous bicyclist, and he wouldn't catch on to the fact that I was the same guy he'd seen before.

I told myself it would be a productive endeavor, no matter the outcome.

I might find out where he lived.

I might learn who his customers were.

Or ... my thoughts halted abruptly when he put on his right-turn signal and turned into a drugstore parking lot. I locked the bike on a bike rack and strode casually inside, making a point to ignore him.

Inside the front door, I watched while pretending to be busy on my phone. The young lady emerged from the car while Pharmer stayed put. She headed toward the back, where the pharmacy was, and I followed, eyes still on my phone. She got into the line with two people ahead of her, and I, thinking fast, loitered near the blood pressure machine where a lady sat, her arm in the cuff.

I gathered Pharm's lady friend was here to fill a prescription. Somehow, I needed to get close enough to hear the conversation.

As luck would have it, she stepped to the window as the woman at the machine finished up. I sat and went through the motions of taking my blood pressure. No, I'm not going to tell you what it was. Suffice it to say, it was elevated, probably due to this exciting yet nerve-racking mission.

"We always recommend talking to the pharmacist when you first go on opioids like OxyContin," I heard the woman behind the counter say. "And this is a rather large order for an initial prescription."

"No, that's okay," Girlfriend said. "My doctor discussed it with me already. He doesn't think I'll need more than a month's supply."

I heard no more as I made a rapid beeline for the men's room. Changing quickly into the Bears jersey, I pressed the other helmet on my head and hurried out of the store, just in time to see Girl get into the car and hand Boy the paper bag.

I quickly put the other shades on and watched from the corner of the store where I'd parked the bike. Pharmer took the bag, then backed out onto the boulevard again.

I set out behind him.

About ten minutes later, he pulled into a different drugstore parking lot, and all three of us repeated the same procedure. Girlfriend got him another bottle of Oxy, then they raced off, with me in my Yosemite shirt and wire-rimmed glasses, fifty feet behind him, with my suspicions proven correct.

I knew now he got his pills. He got them legitimately from local pharmacies and paid for them with our tax dollars. But how did he get three prescriptions written for his lady friend? Pharmacists don't accept prescriptions without proper physician's credentials.

But who, you might ask, is this Pharmer Boy, Steve? You know his MO. Can't you have him arrested?

Very good question. Stay tuned for the sixth and final installment of "That Homeless Life."

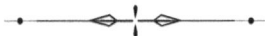

Jon closed the newspaper and picked up his phone. 3:00 already? No reason to stay in this graveyard any longer. But he needed to contact Steve before he headed home.

Hey Steve, good article. Do we get to learn who Pharmer Boy really is?

Hey, Jon. I never learned his real name. But between you and me, his street handle is King-Boy. Quite an egotistical dude.

If you knew his real name, would you alert the cops?

Sure, Jon, but drug dealers are usually released fairly quickly. Don't know if it would do any good unless he gets convicted.

Wish we could exercise a little vigilante justice. Seems it's the only kind in operation right now.

Ha, too true.

If the public knew King-Boy's true identity, no doubt he'd be off to jail before he knew what hit him.

CHAPTER

Thirty-Three

Faith is a fine invention For gentlemen who see; But microscopes are prudent In an emergency!

~Emily Dickinson

Even though his dad had forbidden him to hang out at Ethan's after school, Tanner figured he'd never know. His dad often got home after six. And Tanner couldn't resist those sexy websites Ethan had found.

This afternoon, he and Ethan opened the door to an empty apartment. With Dwyer and the parents at work, and Ethan's sister at her friend's house, the two could watch and dream to their heart's content.

"I have a surprise for you," Ethan said as they entered his room. Ethan closed the door and went to his dresser, where he opened a drawer and took out a tissue. He unwrapped it and held it out. On the tissue sat two little green pills with the number 80 carved into them.

Tanner stepped back. No way was he taking any more of Ethan's drugs. "What's that?"

Ethan thrust the tissue at him. "They're Green Goblins. Here, take one."

He'd heard guys at school talking about those little green OxyContin pills. Weren't those what landed his stepbrother Richard in the hospital? Meg and his dad probably didn't know he'd heard their discussion the other day, but he'd heard enough to know the pills were very bad news.

Backing up two more steps, Tanner held up a palm. "No way." Ethan didn't know he'd ended up in the emergency room the night of the edible, and he couldn't admit to his friend what a lightweight he'd proven to be. He searched his mind for a reasonable excuse. "My dad will kill me if I come home high again." Parents always made great scapegoats.

Scoffing, Ethan popped a pill in his mouth, then swigged a gulp of water. "Fine. You'll be missing out on the best high ever. Ten times better than weed." He bound to his computer and booted it up. Tanner peered over his shoulder, trying to swat the guilt away.

Sure, he liked the girly sites, but at least he didn't do hard drugs. He hoped that counted for something in the eyes of God.

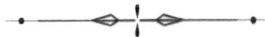

Once in his empty house, Jon hung up his sweater and went in search of Tanner. Fortunately, his son seemed fully recovered from his weed overdose, but Jon still worried.

Tanner's room yawned empty even though he should be home from school by now.

He'd better not be with Ethan.

Picking up his phone, he started to text. Then stopped when a better plan formed in his head.

He grabbed his sweater, beelined to Unit 10 at La Cienega Apartments, and rang the doorbell.

Ethan cursed when the ringing bell echoed down the hall. He slammed his browser closed, cursed again, and reached the bedroom door in two long strides. "Guess I gotta get the door."

"Why?" Tanner seized his arm and pulled him back in. "Just pretend nobody's home."

Ethan shook him off. "No, I need to see if it's the game I ordered. It should've been delivered by now."

He hurried to the front door and opened it.

"Hey, Ethan." Tanner's dad's voice carried clearly through the open door. "Is my son here?"

Tanner cursed silently. Had Dad seen his bike parked at the rack downstairs?

As if he'd read Tanner's mind, Dad said, "I see a bike that looks an awful lot like his. Please go tell him to come to the door."

Ethan didn't dare ignore Dad's no-nonsense tone. Tanner dragged his feet along the hallway to the front door, where Dad loomed.

"Tanner, get your butt home right now."

A quick study of his dad's face, the set jaw, the fiery eyes, told him he was in deep trouble.

He was probably grounded for the next three years.

CHAPTER

Thirty-Four

If I can stop one heart from breaking, I shall not live in vain; If I can ease one life the aching, Or cool one pain, Or help one fainting robin Unto his nest again, I shall not live in vain.

~Emily Dickinson

"Meg." Candy's voice shook. "The strangest thing just happened."

"What?" Meg tossed another roll of paper towels into the grocery cart.

"I went to see BB at the rehab place again, and she refused to see me."

"She actually said that?"

"Not exactly. When I arrived, she was watching TV, and when she saw me, she got up and headed down the hall. Adelle went to tell her she had a visitor, but she couldn't get her to come out of her room. She said BB refused to answer, then went and laid on her bed like she wasn't feeling well. I know BB saw me, but she pretended she didn't."

"Weird." Meg scanned the Walmart card section for a funny-yet-romantic husband birthday card while trying to focus on Candy's words at the same time. She wished she could tell Candy the truth … she didn't have time for this. She needed to get home by five. She and Jon had reservations at Luna Blu for his forty-fifth birthday. "Sounds like she wasn't feeling well."

"She looked just fine when I walked in. I wonder if I said or did something to offend her? But I can't think of a single thing."

Meg picked up a card, scanning the rhyme inside. Ooh, romantic and sexy too. "I doubt you said or did anything wrong. She may have just not been in the mood for company."

"But then, Adelle told me about two other gals who would be out of the program in a week and would need a place to go. I told her okay."

"Which'll be three residents under your roof." She wanted to add, can you handle so many?

Instead, she said, "Candy's House will soon be a full house."

"Yes, it will. I need to apply for more funding, and hopefully, the state will send me some part-time help."

Meg stopped, her attention caught by two teenage sisters she recognized from her church. She waved and smiled, recalling that their parents had founded a non-profit ministry which located Christian homes for young adults aging out of the foster system, homes where caring Christian couples would provide the stability they so desperately needed before launching out into the world. It was no secret adults who'd been raised in foster care struggled far more than others with the responsibilities and demands of adulting.

"It's such an overwhelming need," she heard herself say while her mind spun with ideas.

"Yes, it is. Far more women need shelters than we can accommodate. Ten women live at Casa de Merced right now, all of whom will need a place to go after they get out."

"How many halfway houses are available?"

"In the county? About twenty. Most of them are full right now."

"What is typical in these cases?"

"When residents are finished with the program, the shelter tries to prioritize housing for the women who came from abusive conditions or are pregnant. My home is on the list. The rest typically go live with friends or family, but they're often in unstable or dangerous situations.

Many of the ladies escaped such environments, but too many times, they don't have any choice but to go back to the same situation which created their addiction in the first place."

"How long do the women stay at homes like yours?"

"The outpatient program lasts at least six months. When their time is up, they may or may not have a job or a place to rent. Sometimes they reapply to stay another six months."

"Obviously, we need more stable homes for them, and not just for the pregnant ones."

Candy cleared her throat, her soft voice all at once hoarse. "Not enough homes are available for all of them. We can't keep up with demand. It's why so many end up back on the streets."

Meg, basket in hand, followed the teenage sisters to the self-check line. "Maybe some of the families at church could help. Let me ask around, and I'll let you know."

As she ended the call, the teens' parents approached her, welcoming smiles intact.

"Hey, you two." She received Isabel Pine's shoulder hug and smiled at Isabel's husband, Chris. "You're just the people I need to see right now."

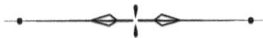

To: SausalitoJon

From: Phleet Powerboats, Portland OR

Hello, Jon,

Thank you for your honesty in declining our offer of employment here in Portland. I understand how important family is, and I don't blame your wife for wanting to stay put.

Down the hall, Tanner's door slammed. Jon's mouth tightened as he visualized his son throwing his backpack on his bed, pouting. *The joys of parenting teenage boys.* Still, he had to stand firm in enforcing the rules. He'd been through similar issues with his older son, and he and Connor had weathered those years just fine.

He returned to Ms. Yates's email, thankful for the positive tone so far. And the fact she'd even bothered to reply. Jon hadn't expected it.

> However, we are very impressed with your credentials and wonder if you would consider joining our team in a different capacity. The Board has been discussing the possibility of expanding our marketing team, and one of the locations under consideration is the Bay Area. Our scouting team scoped out a likely location on Market Street in downtown San Francisco, and with the right person, we could go ahead and get the ball rolling. After seeing samples of the creative promotional campaigns you spearheaded for your business, we envision you as the perfect fit. We'd like to offer you the position of Regional Director of Northern California. Please call me at your earliest convenience to discuss this in more detail.

Jon's eyes widened at the annual salary Ms. Yates proposed. What an answer to prayer. He couldn't wait to tell Meg their offices would be just blocks from each other. They could commute to work together, have lunch in Union Square, or eat dinner at the Wharf.

His mind wandered from one happy scenario to another. He picked up his phone to dial the Portland number, then stopped. *Back up. Not so fast.* His wife came first on his list. He pulled up her number on FaceTime so he could see her expression when he told her the good news.

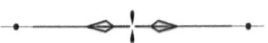

Meg frowned at her phone. "So sorry," she informed her friends. "It's my husband wanting to FaceTime." She approached the self-checkout and set her basket down. "Hi, honey. What's up?"

The crinkles around Jon's eyes lifted—a positive sign. Was it finally their turn for some good news?

"I've got good news and bad. Which do you want first?"

"We're overdue for some good news."

"You should see the job offer I just got. And you'll never guess where."

Her grin matched his as she scanned her purchases with her free hand. "Timbuktu?"

Laughing, he nodded. "You got it. Not. Downtown San Francisco. Regional Director of Northern California with Phleet. It's a new position in a new office."

"Wow, honey. Amazing. Praise the Lord! After such great news, what could be so bad?"

"You're right, the bad news isn't even close. It's about Tanner. I caught him with Ethan today." He filled her in on the afternoon's events until Meg reached her car, where they discussed possible plans of action.

Once at home, she told him about her encounter with the Pines. "They might be able to help with some of the women at Merced. We need to have them and Candy over for dinner to discuss."

"Yes," he said, but she could tell he wasn't really listening. She couldn't blame him. No doubt, visions of a promising new position and a wayward son waged war in his head.

CHAPTER

Thirty-Five

I shall know why, when time is over, And I have ceased to wonder why;
Christ will explain each separate anguish In the fair schoolroom of the sky.

~Emily Dickinson

Myla tucked her legs under herself and held her phone away from the cloudy light filtering through her window, taking advantage of her rare alone time. Her two roommates were occupied—who knows where. She didn't keep tabs on them.

> Had ANOTHER dream about JJ and Bowie. I guess it's JJ's way of keeping his promise to come back and visit me. I asked him what it's like on the other side, but I couldn't hear his answer. His mouth moved, but no sound came out. He still looked scrawny and underfed, though, so I gather it's not much different on the other side than in the tent. And Bowie just looked at me and wagged his tail, like he was glad to see me. Still dunno what happened to that dog. Probably got took to a shelter somewhere. Hope he didn't get put down. :'(JJ would kill me. (Hmm, wouldn't that make a morbid movie. GHOST II – in which dead man kills the girl he loved because she let his beloved dog die. Together they go off into the forevermore, wreaking havoc as a team. Starring Chris Hemsworth and Demi Moore's

daughter, Rumer. When I get out of here, I'm gonna write the screenplay. Ha.)

Night before last, I had a dream that JP found me and called the police to arrest me. Then I woke up. Huge relieved sigh. What a shockeroo if it were real, cuz nobody here knows what I did.

Sucks being wanted by the Popo.

Watched today's required Sober Guy podcast w/ Bestie – check. Lecture, lecture, lecture, but no new information. Will someone please tell me something I don't already know?

She shifted and uncurled her legs, massaging the numb spot on her calf.

The new roomie, Jaynee, is getting mighty tighty with Bestie. Don't know what to make of it. That gurl rubbed me the wrong way from the get-go. What does Roberta see in her? Will Bestie morph into ex-Bestie? Better not. So tired of people coming and going from my life. Will someone please stick around for once?

The baby pushed against her bladder, and she bound from her bed and staggered to the bathroom. With both stalls occupied, she propped herself against the counter and pressed her legs together, clutching her phone as if it could absorb the pressure of the baby's antics.

Seconds later, a toilet flushed, and one of the stalls opened. *Speak of the devil,* as her mom used to say. Jaynee came out, scowling at Myla as if she hated Myla with the same fervency Myla hated her, her hair as frizzed and ratted as always. Didn't she own a hairbrush? Or did she just not care? Myla rushed into the vacated stall just in time.

She heard Jaynee humming softly, then the faucet drowned out the tune. Myla waited while the other woman toweled off. Why was she taking so long?

Finally, the door opened, then closed, and Myla pulled up her jeans. Out of habit, she patted her back pocket.

No phone.

Where was it? A thread of panic seized her.

She darted out, then noticed her phone on the counter. The releasing panic left her limp, and she headed back to her room, her phone cradled in her palm. The journal page lay open. Had Jaynee seen it?

How could she have been so careless?

She'd heard of pregnancy brain. Now she knew what they were talking about.

But the questions fled when the front door opened, and Candy walked in.

Myla groaned, and her blood pressure jumped several notches when she saw the sandwich lady tailing Candy to Adelle's desk to sign in. Even worse, Jon Paulson's wife craned her neck seeking someone, probably her. Of all the people to show up today, why did it have to be Meg Paulson? What did she need to do to get these people off her back?

Oh, no, the sandwich lady saw her. She nudged Candy, but Myla darted into her room and was out of sight before Candy turned.

Maybe she needed to find another place to live. But right now, she'd stay in her room, feigning illness if Adelle hunted her down. Not too difficult, with the four-month-old fetus starting to kick. Not only did Baby like to kick her bladder, but he apparently enjoyed sitting on her stomach.

As she expected, Adelle poked her head in. "You have visitors."

Myla plopped to her side on the hard twin bed, her finger tracing a seam on the taupe comforter. She turned her back on Adelle. "Don't wanna see nobody today."

"What's up with you? It's the nice lady who offered you a place to live when you leave here."

"I just don't feel good." She turned her head to meet Adelle's annoyed grimace. "This baby's worn me out."

"I'm getting tired of making excuses for you." A whoosh of air accompanied Adelle's exit. Myla crept to the door to hear the ensuing conversation, but her room sat three doors away, and all she caught were murmurs. When the front door thudded closed, she hurried to the room next door. Her rock, rehab bestie Roberta, would lend a listening ear.

Of course, Roberta didn't know about her Jon Paulson problem. Nor would she ever. Even though forty-year-old Roberta had done many worse things in her drug-ridden days, she was straight and narrow now and would probably try to talk Myla into turning herself in.

Not gonna happen.

With a script solidifying in her mind, she knocked. No answer. "Yoo-hoo," she called through the cracked-open door.

Myla peeked into the empty room. Maybe she was in the TV room or the dining room. Sure seemed like soft-hearted Roberta was hanging with Jaynee more than with Myla lately.

She passed two more rooms until she reached the empty classroom at the end of the hall. Muffled voices carried through the cracked-open door, and she stepped forward to listen.

Roberta's voice carried clearly. "I have no clue who JP is, and it ain't your business anyway."

Myla clapped a hand to her mouth, her breath coming fast and hard.

"But she's wanted by the police." Jaynee's rasp set her heart pounding. "I'm not a snoop, but hey, her phone was sitting right in front of me. I couldn't help seeing it."

Whirling, Myla hurried to her room and made sure the door latched, and then yanked her backpack off the closet shelf. Breathing hard, she tossed clothing and accessories and books and shoes into it. Jaynee hated Myla, and now she knew Myla hated her. What was to stop her from alerting the police to Myla's whereabouts?

Once all her worldly possessions rested safely inside the pack, only then did she plop to the bed, realizing she had to come up with a plan.

She didn't care what it took. Sure, she'd miss Roberta and Sister Louise, and she hoped they missed her. She'd forfeit her one-month sobriety chip. But she had to get out of here. Now.

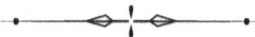

Getting out of my prison was easier than I imagined.

She'd checked to ensure everyone was self-occupied with their free time activities and snuck into the kitchen while Adelle focused on her computer. Her experience with human nature taught her most people are oblivious to details that don't impact themselves, and today, human nature had prevailed. Nobody noticed she had her backpack on. Nobody had stopped her. The kitchen door led into the thrift shop, and after weaving around displays of clothing and household goods, stroller-pushing moms and running toddlers, she'd reached the shop's glass exit door, pushed it open, and boldly stepped out. And it had gone without a hitch.

But now, what would she do? She should have known Tyler wouldn't answer her call. As she trudged along San Rafael's main drag, her backpack heavy on her shoulders, she saw nothing familiar.

But at least the friendly blue cloud-studded sky lifted her spirits. The golden sun's vivid gleam tried to burn joy into her parched soul. Orange poppies smiled at her from cracks in the sidewalk, and the trees waved bright green limbs at her.

For so many years, addiction had draped a gray veil over her five senses. She'd never imagined sobriety could paint the world in such brilliant new hues.

She needed to find a park or vacant lot to set up her tent until she could find a new shelter. One night on the streets couldn't hurt.

Squealing brakes made her dart to a dentist office's graveled yard. "Hey!" she heard. "BB?"

She cursed. How would anyone here know her? A red Honda sat at the curb, and someone called to her through the open window.

It was the preggie lady from NA. The Oxy addict's wife who'd brought the Candy lady to Merced. Meg's daughter-in-law.

She groaned. Too late to run or hide. Kassidy was already getting out.

"BB!" A red flip-flop-clad foot landed on the curb. "Where are you going?"

"Nowhere."

"Are you on your way to the NA meeting? You can ride with us if you want."

Myla turned and threw Kassidy a glare fierce enough to thrust the young woman back to her car. "Don't see why it's any of your business."

"Hey." Her husband stared out the window, eyebrows drawn and angry. "She's just trying to help. You know, we're all in this together. Stop being a b—"

"Rich!" Kassidy, after throwing a reproachful glare over her shoulder, stepped closer to Myla. "Everything okay?"

Myla nodded, willing them with all her might to leave. She turned her back on them until she heard the engine rev.

She hated herself. What kind of person would treat a kind soul like Kassidy with such venom?

Only a wretched addict such as herself.

She lifted her phone and dialed.

Voice mail.

"Tyler? I need help."

CHAPTER

Thirty-Six

Whenever you are asked if you can do a job, tell 'em, 'Certainly I can!'
Then get busy and find out how to do it.

~ Theodore Roosevelt

Meg laid out a tray of shrimp tacos—wrapped with great care and precision by her oh-so-thoughtful husband— on the island between the dining room and kitchen. Jon stood at the kitchen counter and mixed raspberry vinaigrette dressing into the spinach-and-walnut salad while the aroma of rhubarb crisp wafted from the oven.

Jon sniffed. "Honey, we've outdone ourselves. If they don't love this dinner, I'll eat the dishes."

"I love cooking with you. You're a bona fide Gordon Ramsey, my love." Her ex-husband, Phillippe, had hated cooking and let her do it all. At least meal preparation had gotten her mind off BB's strange reaction this afternoon when she and Candy dropped by. For the second time, she'd hid in her room and made some excuse not to see them.

Very odd. But addicts were not known for rational behavior. Had she said or done something to spook the young woman? She shrugged and resolved to try again next week.

The doorbell rang, and Meg opened the door to see Chris and Isabel Pine's smiling faces. Rather, Isabel smiled. Chris, drawn and haggard as though he'd just finished running a marathon, forced a smile, and Meg wondered what had caused his pained expression.

They engaged in small talk around the kitchen island and munched tacos until Chris brought up the reason for their visit. "My wife says you want to know more about our ministry to foster kids."

Meg nodded. "Remind us again of the name."

"Eighteen Candles. It's a 501c3 non-profit."

Isabel swallowed a bite of taco. "We help find support and resources for foster kids who have turned eighteen. For the ones who have dropped out of high school, we get them plugged into GED resources. We can also do job placement and link them with other services like mentoring to ensure they are ready to live as productive citizens."

Jon nodded. "I understand many of them have suffered trauma, like the teen boys at church I've been helping out with for a few years."

"And some of those boys have been through the foster system, haven't they?"

"A few. But most of them are from impoverished homes, single-parent homes, and non-English-speaking homes. Many of them struggle in school. So weekly Game Night is a getaway they look forward to."

Isabel nodded, grinning. "We've noticed how they flock to you on Sunday mornings."

Jon let the compliment slide right by. He was the humblest man Meg had ever known. He asked, "Do you provide your clients with mental health referrals also?"

"It's one of the things we offer. But we can't force them."

"If they decide to go to community college or trade schools," Chris added, "we help them with the financial aid process."

"Sounds like a wonderful ministry," said Meg. "Jon does similar things for his boys. I looked at your website. I'm impressed by the number of success stories you've achieved."

"The Lord has blessed the ministry big-time," said Isabel. "So many problems have been avoided because of 18 Candles' intervention. Those kids are cursed with bad odds." She held up her phone. "I want to show you a photo of Morgan. She's one of our successes." A pretty blonde smiled on Isabel's screen. "She's attending medical school at Loma Linda. Three-point-five GPA. Yet she barely graduated from high school. If the ministry hadn't found her, who knows where she'd be now."

Meg smiled. "How do you find the kids you mentor?"

"We have a vast network of foster parents throughout the state." Isabel set the phone face-up beside her to keep Morgan's photo visible. "We contact them, or they reach out to us. Or sometimes the kids do, at least the more self-motivated ones."

"What about Morgan?" Meg nodded toward the photo. "How did she hook up with your team?"

"Her foster mom reached out to us when Morgan was a junior, hoping we could do something to motivate her. We got her some mentoring and tutoring, which seemed to help. She seemed to have no awareness of what the real world was going to require of her and how she could prepare herself for it." Isabel shook her head. "So much bad parenting. It just breaks my heart."

"Too many parents are incarcerated or addicted to alcohol or drugs themselves," Chris added, looking even more tightly wound. "Plus, the less-than-ideal foster parents are only in it to collect money from the state. Poor parenting can contribute to kids' future homelessness."

A vision of the Bunkert home loomed in Meg's mind. She wiped her fingers on her napkin. "Does your organization do any homeless outreach?"

"It's not something we've felt led to do." Chris picked up the last taco and examined it, his forehead creases deepening as if he had something heavy weighing on his mind. "Several ministries already exist for that niche, and we've always felt the Lord led us to focus on this one demographic. In an indirect way, we're working to prevent it."

Isabel traced a thin finger along the Formica pattern. "These young adults aging out of foster care are so vulnerable. They're just one bad break from landing on the street."

Chris nodded. "Meg, my wife said you're specifically concerned about a young woman at Casa de Merced who's pregnant."

Meg, pulling the warm cobbler from the oven, nodded and dished up four servings. By the time she finished telling them about her history with BB, the dessert was gone. "But now she refuses to see Candy and me when we visit." She started to stack empty plates—her hands slightly shaky from the intensity of the conversation. "It's very strange. She originally agreed to stay at Candy's when her ninety days are up, but then she backed out. I wondered if you guys might know of other places she could go."

Jon followed her to the sink with the rest of the dishes as Isabel placed her finger to her mouth in thought.

"I'm sure we can come up with some names. But Casa de Merced will already have a network of homes they use."

Still, Meg somehow felt responsible for the girl. Maybe because she was vested in her recovery? Dismissing the pondering for later, she beckoned the others into the living room. She and Jon held hands on the brown vinyl loveseat while Chris and Isabel settled on the matching sofa. Chris crossed his legs, ankle on knee. "We have another matter on our minds we'd like to discuss with you."

"We're listening."

"We are retiring at the end of this year."

Surprised, Meg raised her brows. Neither of them appeared anywhere near retirement age.

Isabel noticed Meg's reaction. "Maybe retiring isn't the right term. We're stepping down, which means an important vacancy will open up very soon for a married couple with a heart for ministry."

Meg could see where this was going. Before she could ask more questions, Chris began to speak.

"I was diagnosed with Stage 3 colon cancer last week. I start chemo Monday."

Meg reached for Isabel's hand. Now she understood Chris's troubled air. "Oh, I'm so, so sorry."

Isabel's blue eyes dampened. "We have a grueling fight ahead of us. The ministry will have to go on without us. Our daughters need us more than ever now."

Chris rubbed his wife's shoulder. "And we need them."

Clutching Meg's hand, Isabel wiped at a tear with her free hand. "The ministry runs best with a married couple in charge. Currently, Chris ministers to the guys, and I take the women under my wing. And Meg, when we talked at Walmart the other night, it was like God was whispering to me about you two."

"Really?"

Isabel nodded. "Yes, when you were telling me about the ministries you two have been involved in."

Chris leaned forward. "Jon, you two met while you were the leader of a support group, I understand."

Jon smiled over at Meg. "Yes, FOGY, a group for people with gay family members. It didn't take me long to realize I wanted to get to know her."

Warmth snaked through Meg's heart at the memories. What a testimony to God's goodness, blessing her with a man like Jon.

Isabel shifted. "Are you still considering selling your business?"

"I am." Jon met Meg's gaze as awareness dawned on him. "But I have …"

"Would you two consider stepping in?" Chris wasted no time getting to the point. He named an annual salary at about half Meg and Jon's current gross pay. "God laid you two on our hearts. We see how much you care about the disadvantaged, and because of your experience, we think you'll be perfect for the job."

Meg searched Jon's response. Did she see a flash of dismay—and guilt—flitting across his features?

What was God doing? With Jon's new six-figure position practically thrust in his lap, would he even consider running a Christian non-profit for half the salary?

"Well …" Jon watched as he ran his thumb across Meg's palm, back and forth, reflecting his agitated mindset. "I actually was offered a new job today." As he recapped the offer, Meg sensed the disappointment in their new friends. "Have you started the recruiting process yet?"

"We've just started."

Jon turned to Meg. "Hey, what about Bill and Camille?"

Meg turned to the Pines. "You know them, right? From church?"

"Yes, the couple you two hang out with," said Isabel. "We've seen them. You feel they'd be good for this ministry?"

Jon nodded. "They're great people and love the Lord."

The Pines agreed to contact the Pattersons, and they took their leave shortly after. Meg watched them fold themselves into their blue Prius.

"I'd better give Camille a heads-up. Hope she doesn't get upset we sloughed them off on her."

"I hated saying no to them. They mean well. But how can they think God steered them to us? Seems to me He already made His will clear."

CHAPTER

Thirty-Seven

I stepped from plank to plank So slow and cautiously; The stars about my head I felt, About my feet the sea. I knew not but the next Would be my final inch,—This gave me that precarious gait Some call experience.

~Emily Dickinson

Sometimes, Meg had discovered, God spoke to her while she stood heart-deep in painting. As she stood poised before her easel, paintbrush in hand, she prayed this would be one of those times.

God, what are you trying to tell me?

A vision of runaway foster kids—empty-eyed, emaciated—rose into her mind. She picked up a brush and scrutinized her palette, then mixed a dab of Brown Ochre with a touch of Indian Yellow, hoping to achieve a realistic skin tone.

"God, show us Your will." She outlined a face first, then added a shapely mouth of pale Terra Rose. "Those poor kids." Had BB been a foster kid? She squinted, trying to remember BB's eye color, and added two Burnt Sienna eyes. "I sense Jon is being swayed by the money, Lord." She hadn't told him how her heart had resonated at the stories the Pines told, but she needed to be honest with him. She couldn't see Bill as a suitable choice to co-lead such a ministry, not like people-loving, gregarious Jon, whose ability to persuade and influence came so naturally.

Stepping back from the easel, she studied the unfinished portrait. Yes, she'd captured BB's essence—the round Betty Boop eyes, the shock of unruly hair as white and coarse as a polar bear's coat. *BB*, she whispered. Not for the first time, she wondered about the girl's real name. Why hadn't she thought to ask Adelle? But was Adelle, bound by rules of confidentiality, even free to tell her?

Her cell rang, and the brush swiped a startled sienna streak across the face. *Oops. At least it's fixable.* "Hi, Kassidy."

"Meg, hi! Did you get my texts?"

"Your texts?"

The screen lit with two new notifications.

CALL ME.

Meg, call me!!

"So sorry, Sid. We had company for dinner, and I didn't see them. What's up?"

"You won't believe who I saw today." Meg's jaw dropped at the story of a runaway BB. She picked up another brush and began filling in facial details with her free hand. The face slowly took shape as she visualized BB, frantic in her haste to escape but instead being swallowed up by the hard-core life on the streets. Why would she throw away her fragile, hard-fought sobriety? What had made her run?

"Kassidy? What time?"

"Rich and I were driving to a three o'clock NA meeting."

Her mind whirled, doing the math. She and Camille had gone to see BB somewhere between two and two-thirty. Coincidence? Because it didn't make sense she'd leave the shelter so abruptly.

Where could the poor girl have gone? How could the streets be more desirable than a warm bed with a roof over one's head?

Had she, Meg, played a role in the girl's escape?

But she couldn't think of a single thing she'd done. A sense of urgency gripped her. She needed to know BB's real name, not only because she felt responsible for the girl but because she could be in danger. *Betty Boop. Ms. Elizabeth M. Boop, Missing and Endangered.*

"Sid, thanks for telling me. I'll call Adelle and find out what's going on."

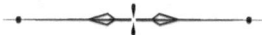

Myla sat in Starbucks and waited for her phone to beep. Late afternoon sun slanted through the tall windows. She propped her sore feet on a chair, feeling like she'd trudged for hours. Maybe only one. In less than two hours, this place would close for the day, and she didn't know this part of San Rafael. Nor had she heard back from Tyler. Was he ghosting her like King-Boy did?

She might as well order coffee while she waited. Pulling a couple of crumpled bills from her pocket, she approached the counter.

"Can I help you?" A young man with black curly hair flashed a smile at her.

Hmm, what a looker. She couldn't help returning his grin. "I'm dying for the most excellent cup of coffee I can find. What do you recommend?"

"I like a straight black coffee." His alert dark eyes twinkled. "It's my favorite because I love the taste of coffee. Anyone who's a coffee drinker knows exactly what I mean."

She nodded with a glance at his name badge. "Thank you for the tip, Mateo C. Maybe I can return the favor sometime." Her grin stretched wider.

"Well, you never can tell." He winked, then turned and handed her a medium black coffee. "Enjoy."

She'd missed the flirtations and giddy feelings from male attention. She chose a table within Mateo's view and picked up a newspaper folded haphazardly on a nearby table. It had been way too long since she'd kept up with the news. She reached for the paper and noted the date—two days ago. A headline caught her eye:

THAT HOMELESS LIFE
by Steve Davis

PART 5 OF A 6-PART SERIES

"You can lead a horse to water, as they say. But you can't make it drink. You can open homeless shelters and build affordable housing, but you can't make them go."

This guy is right on. Some of her fellow campers had been offered nice apartments in soon-to-be-built new complexes, but they'd said no. They liked the unstructured freedom of life on the streets, a place of no accountability. She sipped the coffee—rich, delicious, smoky.

"Many of you probably believe if we just had enough affordable housing or opened more homeless shelters, we could get those people off the street. After a week in a homeless camp, I can assure you this is not the case."

What? He'd spent a week in a homeless camp? On purpose?

"In a week full of surprises, the shattering of this common belief sits near the top. 'But Steve,' I hear you thinking. 'Why would anyone willingly live in such horrid conditions if they have other options?' "

Maybe because the other options are more horrid than you think?

"When you live in a drugged stupor 24/7, you don't notice your surroundings. The high inside you feels so good—nothing else matters."

How does this guy know so much about camp life after only a week? And who was he to judge addiction? Had he ever lived through the skin-crawling craving, the obsessive compulsion of the long-term addict? Had he experienced dopesickness?

She kept reading, enjoying the best cup of coffee she'd had in a long time. Casa de Merced had served coffee so weak it was practically see-through. Riveted by the reporter's account of trailing the drug dealer and his new girlfriend like some undercover detective, she chuckled. *Pharmer Boy, huh? More like King-Boy, but you're not about to expose him, are you?*

Maybe she should expose him. He'd fed her addiction, used her, got her pregnant, then ghosted her. And now she knew why…he'd replaced her. She knew his real name and where he lived. She could call the cops right now…

Her mind tugged her back to the days after Tyler tried to make her abort their baby. After he cast her away like she was nothing more than an STD, his stepson stepped into the gap with comfort and then some. He showed up to give moral support, holding her hand during Lamaze class as if atoning for his stepfather's sins.

She wished she'd realized the truth hidden behind his caring persona, a caring which only lasted until she found herself pregnant again. Even though Tyler and King-Boy weren't blood-related, they might as well have been. They were cut from the same self-serving cloth.

She regretted telling King-Boy she was pregnant with his baby. He deserved to get arrested for vandalism and drug dealing.

Her phone beeped. Tyler, finally. *I'm sorry I can't get away to help you right now. Here's a hotline # you can call…*

She opened Zinnia and typed.

> SMH. DJ thinks a hotline number is all I need. He "can't get away" sez he. Oh, and there's this reporter who's on King-Boy's trail and even wrote about it in the paper! You go, boy. I hope KB sees it and it makes him sweat a little. Maybe he'll be sorry for all his dirty deeds…not. Or sorry he replaced me so easily. Debating whether to sic popo on him. But he'd know it was me.

She shivered, remembering the blackness in his eyes, the lack of regard for anyone but KB, and once more lifted her phone.

On the other hand I ought to sic the cops on DJ. It was thanks to him I ended up a sidewalk-camping dope addict, thanks to him I lost my baby....Naw. He'd deny everything. Who would believe me?

She set the phone in her pocket and hoisted her backpack. Time to find a quiet corner somewhere she could pitch her tent and get in a few hours of dreaming.

"Leaving already?" Mateo smiled down at her.

"Well ..." She returned to her seat, setting her pack down, flashing her friendliest smile. "Not if I can have some company."

"I'm happy to keep you company, especially if it means you'll stay for a while." He grinned.

Stay cool. "Won't you get in trouble?"

"I'm on my break. I can keep you company for exactly ten minutes." He nodded at the steaming cup between them. "How's the coffee?"

"The tastiest ever."

He hesitated. "Can I get you another one?"

She preferred him to sit and talk to her. "In a bit. Have a seat."

He sat and gestured at the paper. "Anything good?"

"Just old news." She put the paper on the chair, out of his sight. "How long have you worked here?"

"About a year. I live down the block, so it's handy. What about you?"

Might as well be honest. What did she have to lose? She didn't know this guy from Adam, and he didn't know her from Eve. "I'm currently between homes, to be honest. I've been living out of a tent until I can find a place."

"Really?"

"Because, you know, rents."

"I do know. Mine is outrageous, even with two roommates." He drummed the table with both hands. "If you don't mind my asking, how did you end up houseless?"

"Long story. How much time do you have?"

He glanced at the clock on the wall. "I'll be done in an hour. And then I'll have as much time as you need."

"You're on." She sipped her drink, already antsy for the six o'clock hour. "I'll be outside."

CHAPTER

Thirty-Eight

A wise son maketh a glad father.

Proverbs 10:1

Meg heard Jon's oldest son shout, "Hello?" before she saw him poke his head into her she-shed. She stepped away from the easel.

"Connor?" She greeted him with a hug. "What are you doing here?"

"Left some tools here." Sunlight from the little window reflected off his dark hair as he glanced around at the walls dotted with her paintings. "Do you know what happened to the toolbox I used to keep out here?"

"Check the garage. Jo—Your dad moved everything out of here a few months ago."

The easel now commanded his full attention. "So I see. You paint out here now?"

"I do." She moved to block his view of BB's portrait. She wasn't ready to show anyone. "Hey, how's the new apartment working out?"

"Expensive." He shifted, trying to see the easel as she stood knocking the paintbrush handle against her palm—over and over.

"You like living in Berzerkely?" She grinned at him, but he craned around her, ignoring her invisible barrier.

"Yeah. Whatcha working on?"

Giving up, she stepped aside. Apparently, he wasn't going to leave until she showed him her work in progress. "It's not finished."

"No worries. Your talent comes through no matter what stage you're at." When he saw the unfinished face, a spasm twisted his mouth. "Whoa."

"What do you mean, whoa?"

He shook his head, pointing. "Why are you painting Myla Delaney?"

"Huh?" She couldn't have heard right. "That's not Myla. Her name is BB."

"BB, right. Stands for Betty Boop. Myla's nickname."

As the import of what he was saying sunk in with a heavy thud, her heart started beating again. "BB is Myla? Myla is BB?"

"How do *you* know her?" Connor's tone was almost accusatory.

"BB?" She pointed her brush at the nearly completed portrait. "She's a homeless woman I met recently. She went into rehab, and now she's run off again."

"Figures."

"If BB is Myla ..." she closed her eyes, visualizing Casa de Merced, the skittish way BB darted into her room, "and she was the person who vandalized the shop, she may have known who I was—"

"Vandalized the shop?" Connor's brows drew into a bewildered crease. "How can ..."

"Your dad believes she's the responsible party."

Shaking his head, Connor reached for the doorknob. "Guess I need to go talk to him, then."

He stalked off, and once she'd recovered from the earthquake of a revelation, Meg put down her brush and followed. After Jon heard what his son had to say, the three of them returned to the shed. "Wow." Jon expelled a breath. "It sure looks like Myla. A skinny, goth Myla." He scratched his head as though he couldn't decide how to feel about it. "Do you mean to tell me, all this time we were searching for the same person?"

"She was apparently right under our noses the whole time, Honey."

Jon turned to his son, whose face still hadn't unfrozen. "Connor, how well did you know her?"

The question shook Connor out of his stupor. He thrust his hands into his jeans pockets, keys clanging as if the subject made him nervous. "In high school, I knew her well. We both played percussion in band."

Meg recalled Tanner's claiming Connor liked Myla. Judging by Connor's red cheeks, Tanner nailed it. "You must've hung out after graduation."

"I don't think she graduated."

"What did you think of her?"

An odd expression crossed his face, wiping away the blush. "Nice girl. Funny. Not the vandalizing type."

"I don't remember you ever talking about her until the job came up. Did you know anything about her family?"

Connor plopped onto a stool, his knee jostling. "Well, she didn't really have one. She was in a foster home all through high school."

Meg felt, more than saw, Jon's stunned reaction, and he met her eyes over Connor's head, raising his brows as though he knew exactly what she was thinking.

Why does the subject of foster kids keep coming up?

Turning back to his son, Jon said, "Funny she never mentioned it when she worked for me. Where did she live after high school?"

"I got the impression she was staying with her biological mom. But I'm not sure. Like I said before, she quit replying to my texts."

Silence fell as they all chewed on their thoughts. Meg tilted her head at the portrait. She'd captured the lost little foster girl in the slant of the eyes and the set of her mouth. Yes, she must've lived a hard life. It must have hurt to be thrust from her family into strangers' homes. But did it justify the enormous damage she'd inflicted on Jon and his clients? His entire life's ambition? His father's bequest?

She stepped to her husband's side and slid her arm around his back. "What now, my love?"

He smiled down at her, but his eyes glinted with steel. "I have an idea brewing in my noggin. I think you'll like this."

CHAPTER

Thirty-Nine

You may tie my hands with chains and my feet with shackles, And put me in the dark prison, But you shall not enslave my thinking, For it is free, Like the breeze in the spacious sky.

~Kahlil Gibran

Myla heard Mateo's curse before he poked his head into the closet, where she wrestled a pair of boots over her leggings. "What?"

"What the heck did you do?" He thrust his phone at her.

"Whatcha talking about?" She drew back at her own face staring at her. The caption below: IF YOU KNOW THIS WOMAN'S WHEREABOUTS, PLEASE CONTACT DETECTIVE KENNETH TUCKER AT THE FOLLOWING NUMBER.

The trembling began in her belly and raced up her spine. "Where did you find this?"

"It's all over Facebook. How come you're wanted by the police?"

Her mind scrambled for an answer as her heart madly raced. Mateo's dark eyes drilled holes into her, and she backed away from the force of them. She'd been here just two days, and he and his roommates had been nothing but kind, letting her crash on their sofa and eat their food. Pregnancy truly had its advantages.

And now it was ruined. Silently, she cursed Jon Paulson for hiring a sketch artist.

Mateo wrested his phone from her hand. Out on the street, a car roared by. And she still didn't know what to say.

"No wonder you were on the run." One step closer, and a whiff of ground roast floated at her. This time she stood her ground. She wouldn't let him intimidate her with his coffee breath and fierce gaze. "But you never told me the real reason. What'd you do? Steal a car? Rob a bank? Kill someone?"

"No!" She let loose the swear words turning her head into a pressure cooker. "They think I broke into a place, which is why I had to move on. I didn't do it, but it's my word against theirs." How easily the lie slipped out. The baby launched a painful kick to her ribs as if punishing her for her sin. She doubled over, grimacing.

"Did I drag myself into trouble with the cops by letting you stay here?" Mateo finally stepped back, and, straightening her shoulders, she pulled a deep breath of musty closet air into her lungs.

"Not if you keep your mouth shut."

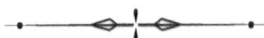

Her long-time high school bestie was going to be so surprised to hear from her. *Bhree, it's me! Long time, no see!* Myla turned away from Mateo's house and trudged east along the boulevard.

At Starbucks, she crossed the street so Mateo wouldn't see her. She hadn't told him goodbye. He didn't know she'd left. Wouldn't he be shocked to find her gone when he got home tonight?

Her phone beeped. Bhree! *Myla??? What the hey? Where'd you disappear to? It's like you dropped off the face of the earth!!*

Tell ya later. At the crosswalk, Myla punched the WALK button.
Do you still live in Pinole? I'm in San Rafael. Can you meet me here?
Can you Uber over here?
Nope, no $. Please, I gotta see U.
Um, ok. Working right now. Traffic's sucking. Six tonight?

She crossed Main Street and headed to the library. *K. Meet me at the café across the street from the big library. See you then!!*

Can't wait to see ya, GF!!

The first thing Myla noticed when Bhree walked in were her dreadlocks. "You look fabu! Love the dreads." The second was her black BLM tee, its bottom hem brushing against a navel ring.

"Big hug! Big hug!" Bhree squealed. She followed with an actual tight squeeze around Myla's shoulders. "Oh, I've missed you so much." She stepped back to give Myla a head-to-toe assessment, then raised her brows as she patted Myla's baby bump. "Do I see a preggo belly?"

"You do."

"Last time we met up, you were six months preggo." She bent side to side, examining the space around Myla as if expecting to see a non-existent child. "And that was over a year ago."

Myla swallowed hard and allowed her twisted scowl to send a silent communiqué to her friend: *Topic off-limits.* She didn't want to embarrass herself with the cracked and broken voice she used every time she mentioned her dead daughter.

Still, Bhree deserved an answer. She cleared her throat—roughly. "Stillborn."

Bhree's lips pursed. "Ah, girlie. I'm so sorry."

Myla shrugged. "Whatevs."

Grasping her arm, Bhree directed her to a table by the window. "C'mon, sit. Tell me everything."

The sun sat low on the horizon by the time Myla finished recapping her year, omitting her law-breaking spree. Bhree pulled her jaw back into place and gripped Myla's forearm. "So, *so* glad you got clean. But I can't believe you left the rehab place just 'cuz someone read your journal. Why'd ya go and do that?"

"She hated me and tried to turn my sponsor against me. Had to get outta there."

"How long you been clean now?"

"Long enough for it to stick."

"You ain't got no money, no place to live. Whatcha gonna do?"

Myla shrugged, hoping her friend took the hint.

Bhree lit up with an idea. "I know one way you could get a wad of dough." She tilted her head. "Don't look at me like that. It's not what you're thinking, girl."

"Then what?"

"Take that baby daddy to court."

"Who, DJ?"

"Yeah. You were seventeen. And he's, what? Thirty-something? It was statutory rape."

"Yeah, the nun at the rehab center said the same thing. She gave me the names of some legal centers that help low-income people."

"Well, there ya go."

"I don't think it's quite so easy, though. He's got more than enough money for the best of lawyers."

Bhree stood and beckoned. "C'mon, let's go back to my place. I have two roommates, and one of them is a pre-law student at Cal. We can ask him what he thinks."

"Can I crash at your place?"

"Sure, if you don't mind sleeping on an air mattress. It's all I got."

So far, Bhree'd said nothing about the Facebook post with Myla's sketch. If she was lucky, Mateo had exaggerated the extent of the post's reach. And most people who knew the old Myla might not recognize her new look. If she were lucky, most people would scroll right on by.

But wait a minute. The composite was how she looked now. Why wouldn't Jon Paulson have described her appearance when he knew her? How would he know she cut her hair and lost all that weight?

Maybe it wasn't Jon who orchestrated the composite. It must have been someone in the homeless camp, like Creepy Dad.

No—Jaynee! She must have called the police! Myla'd got out of there just in time. Someday, she was gonna hunt Jaynee Gurl down and make her pay.

They were halfway across the Bay Bridge before Bhree's tirade against Tyler finally wound down. Myla couldn't help oohing and aahing over the view of the glorious bay at dusk, lights flickering across its rugged hills. It had been so long since she'd seen the bay from this vantage point.

In fact, Tyler had been the last person she'd been with on this bridge, at this very spot. As the water surged below, they'd whizzed past other vehicles as Tyler sped from the abortion clinic because she'd refused to terminate her pregnancy. She still remembered the angry vein pulsing in his temple, the way she gripped the door handle, ready to jump out at the slightest hint of physical retaliation from him.

As it turned out, he'd merely dropped her at her bio mother's Richmond duplex in icy disapproval, and she'd stayed until Lula was born. Until she fell over the cliff.

Grateful to her friend for the rescue, she mentally patted herself on the back for taking a leap of faith and calling Bhree. Who knew? Perhaps her friend could be instrumental in bringing Tyler to justice.

Maybe God existed after all.

CHAPTER

Forty

"Didn't the pastor's sermon on Demas speak to you at all?" Meg studied Jon's profile as he drove them home from church.

"You mean, do I think Demas abandoning Paul because he loved the world is the same as me taking a job with Phleet instead of 18 Candles? Not at all. I'm not walking away from ministry. Would it make you happy if I agreed to support the ministry financially with my God-ordained pay increase? Ministry doesn't have to mean taking over the leadership of the whole shebang."

Apparently, the conviction she'd felt hadn't been passed on to her husband. Her meaningful looks hadn't meant a thing to him. He hadn't felt God's gentle nudge during the post-service conversation they'd had with Isabel regarding the impending closure of 18 Candles. *God, why speak to me and not Jon? He's the one who needed to hear this.*

"But if it closes because the Pines don't find qualified replacements, there won't be a ministry to support. Bill and Camille can't do it."

"Oh, I doubt it will really close." Jon drummed his fingers on the steering wheel. "They'll find someone qualified. I don't know why they think we're their only hope." He braked at a red light, then turned to her. "Sounds like you don't mind kissing two-hundred-grand a year goodbye. Really?"

Did she? Jon's salary from Phleet would keep them living comfortably for many years. But was it God's will for them? Hadn't Jesus made himself clear on how unimportant personal comfort was in the lives of His followers?

As emotions battled their way through her heart, she pondered the story of Demas. "For Demas hath forsaken me, having loved this present world," the pastor read this morning from Second Timothy, then went on to explain how Demas had proved himself an unfaithful disciple. A pang had pierced her heart. Did God see her and Jon as unfaithful? Had Demas been distracted by a shiny lucrative career also? She'd watched for Jon's reaction, but he hadn't flinched. Apparently, he didn't relate the story to himself.

Yet she knew Jon's heart; he had only the highest of motives whenever he made a decision…whatever was best for his family. Obviously, he considered a six-figure job better for them than a demanding ministry position paying less than half of that between the two of them.

She needed to be honest. "I was looking forward to the career change for myself. I've been at my job so long I could do it in my sleep. And I was thinking how great it would be to serve the Lord together."

"We could serve the Lord together by mentoring a foster child." He reached over and covered her hand. She relished the solid weight on hers. "I've been feeling the Lord tugging at my heart for a while now, telling me I can do more to help kids. Mentoring is something we can do together."

Out the windshield, the street sloped gently upward, crowned by a wooded hillside like a woolen cap. She loved this area, one of the most beautiful in the state, and thanked the Lord every morning for the privilege of living here and for arranging circumstances allowing Jon to stay. The prospect of moving out of state had shaken her and made her realize how deep her roots grew here.

And now, after all God's finagling to keep them here, did He have still more finagling up His omniscient sleeve?

"Okay, honey, we can pray about mentoring." She closed her eyes in contemplation. "Maybe that's how He's leading us, after all."

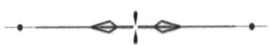

Bhree lived in a tiny, two-bedroom apartment in Pinole with her boyfriend, Miguel, who lounged on the sofa and lifted his beer can at her when Bhree introduced them. The second bedroom belonged to the pre-law roommate, who wasn't home.

After Bhree kicked Miguel off the sofa to set up a makeshift bed for Myla, she wondered if she should ask Bhree how thin the walls were. She didn't need to hear couples getting amorous tonight.

But first things first. Those Marin Mercury articles on homelessness called her name. Steve Davis's excursion into the dregs of humanity intrigued her when she read his fifth installment the other night. The night she met Mateo. She needed to see what else Mr. Davis wrote about people like her. She wondered if she'd met him. She remembered a couple of guys who'd shown up unexpectedly and didn't stay long. They'd been cleaner and better groomed than most. Rookies, apparently. Not caked with grime and hopelessness like the lifers.

She found an empty corner of the living room where she could browse while Bhree and Miguel streamed a movie on Netflix. Anchoring her backpack between herself and the wall, she blocked out the dialog and background noise and found the site.

THE MARIN MERCURY

THAT HOMELESS LIFE
by Steve Davis

PART 1 OF A 6-PART SERIES

You approach the tattered tent city cautiously, careful to avoid the needles and human waste on the sidewalk. You notice cars packed to the gills, in varying degrees of degeneration, parked haphazardly on the sidewalk. Graffiti covers most available surfaces. Shabbily dressed people mill about with apparently nothing productive to do, and you can't help wondering, who are these people, and how did they end up living like third-world citizens here in the wealthiest nation on Planet Earth?

In this six-part series, I tell the story of how I experienced life for myself as an undercover resident in one of Marin County's many homeless camps, whose location will remain confidential.

It's no secret the homeless sweeps in San Francisco have displaced many homeless citizens and have spilled over into our communities here in Marin County. Last week, a Sausalito businessman's shop was severely vandalized shortly after a homeless community set up camp across the parking lot. His business is virtually ruined, and he fears he has lost everything. Although he has no solid proof, he can't help wondering if someone, or a few someones, from the camp might have had something to do with it.

She should have known she couldn't outrun the shame of public exposure. Curses upon Steve Davis and Jon Paulson and his wife the Sandwich Lady and Jaynee Gurl and DJ and King-Boy and…

"Hey, girlfriend?" Bhree, arms akimbo, scrunched her face. "What up with you?"

She sniffed. She'd been shouting curse words and freaking her friend out. Tears slipped down her cheek. From the sofa, Miguel observed, wary and watchful.

The power of her destructive tendencies hadn't hit her until she saw it in black and white.

"Sorry." She wiped her face with the heel of her palm. "Just reading something. Don't worry about me. I'll be fine."

"O-kay." Bhree regarded her for a moment before returning to the couch. Myla clicked Steve Davis's contact link and, after a moment of thought, composed a message with her BettyBoop email as the confirmation address.

Dear Mr. Davis, You don't know me, but the Sausalito businessman you mentioned does. If you have a way to contact him, please tell him I'm very sorry for what I did. He'll know what you're talking about. - BB

She visualized Jon Paulson when he received her message, and her mouth twisted in a half-grin mixed with the salty taste of tears.

Further down the page, she nearly missed a one-paragraph article about a recent accident but did a double take when she spied a familiar name.

Yesterday's traffic fatality marks the fiftieth pedestrian death in the county this year. A homeless woman, Bernice Stoops, lost her life on Bridgeway in Sausalito when she stepped in front of a silver Hyundai. The driver, 53-year-old Edgar Gonzalez, stopped at the scene and cooperated with the authorities.

Aw, poor Mom. She'd been good to Myla. An overall decent person. Too good for Dad. Too bad it wasn't him instead.

CHAPTER

Forty-One

Who would refuse an invitation to such a shining adventure?

~Amelia Earhart

"We're here to interview as volunteer mentors," Jon told the interim director of 18 Candles, a man named Jeffrey, whom Isabel introduced as her brother. Jeffrey sat across from them at a battered desk formerly used by Chris. Haphazard piles of folders threatened to tip off the side. Jon wondered if Jeffrey and Isabel had an assistant to help with administrative tasks.

"Hello, Jon and Meg Paulson." Jeffrey craned at the computer screen, then scowled at the keyboard. He hunt-and-pecked the keys as Jon read the organization's motto stenciled on the wall behind Jeffrey. *Eighteen Candles—Investing in Your Future.*

Pretty vague for a mission statement.

Twenty seconds later, a silence laden with agitated breaths from Jeffrey and questioning glances from Meg ended when Jeffrey spoke. "Here it is. Got your resume right here. Looks really good, Mr. Paulson. Lots of solid experience working with kids already."

Jon nodded. "I enjoy investing in kids' lives."

Jeffrey's elbow knocked a stack of folders onto the floor. "Oops. Dangit. I hate when that happens. I need some time to get those filed, but it seems the time never comes. Glad I'm not here to stay. I'm way too happy to turn this mess over to someone else."

The folders and pages lay strewn on the floor. Jon wanted to ask if he'd considered a digital filing system. In the meantime, this place could use someone to take care of the paperwork. Jeffrey jumped in as though he'd read his mind. "Wish I could bring another person on board. Isabel's been doing the filing, but she's phasing out. Spending time with Chris, you know. I need to find a good office girl."

Jon sensed Meg trying not to roll her eyes at the dated term *office girl*. He could almost hear her thinking, "What is this, nineteen seventy?"

"But it's a moot point anyway," Jeffrey said. "The ministry doesn't have the funds to take on more staff."

How about seeking more donors? Have you thought about applying for grants? He felt Meg's gaze but didn't reciprocate, knowing she would read his thoughts.

Jeffrey clicked his tongue in frustration. Jon decided to keep his mouth shut and let talkative Jeffrey keep going.

"Sorry. I'm trying to print out your mentor packet with your student's info, but this stupid software is driving me crazy. Too complicated. Why can't things happen with one click? I shouldn't have to build a spaceship just to print some pages. Know what I mean?"

Jon nodded. *It's not rocket science.* "Yeah, software can be a bear." He used consultants to troubleshoot his. But no need to say so to Jeffrey. He'd undoubtedly say the ministry couldn't afford consultants.

He wondered who did the bookkeeping. His guess would be Isabel. Most small non-profits had no need for a full-time bookkeeper. But if they couldn't raise enough funds, they'd soon have no books to keep.

The printer whirred, and pages fed through one at a time with excruciating slowness onto the tray. Jeffrey snatched them up, and then felt around on his desk. "Now, where's that stapler? It was just here."

Meg pointed. "Behind you."

He whirled to a cluttered credenza. "Oh yeah. There it is." He stapled the pages and handed them to Meg, who flipped through them.

"Does your printer have a two-sided function?" Jon asked, in case Jeffrey was interested in saving trees.

"Nope, don't think so."

Chalk up another much-needed upgrade. This place screamed "obsolete." How had Chris and Isabel managed? Their strengths obviously lay in the human relationships side of the ministry, and the needed administrative functions must have suffered.

On the drive home, Jon and Meg shared a chuckle. "I believe Mr. Jeffrey Andersen was the most incompetent director I've ever met." Jon smiled at his wife's amusement. "Don't you think?"

She grew serious. "I agree. But it's clear he knows he's not the right guy for the job. Still, the new leaders are going to have excel at cleaning up messes—"

"Implementing necessary upgrades—"

"While still maintaining servant hearts."

"If I ran that place, the first thing I'd do is come up with a better mission statement. Then I'd hire a temp to get all the filing done. I'd update the hardware and software, add a couple of office assistants, and hire consultants. Which means finding creative ways to attract new donors …"

His words trailed off as heavy silence fell over them. Sensing Meg's scrutiny, a funny feeling snaked into his heart. He maintained a respectable distance from the bright yellow school bus in front of him where a child stared out the back window, waving. Jon waved back, seeing but not seeing the houses and businesses on either side, the bay in the distance, and the red brake lights of snarled traffic.

His wife had always been good—too good—at getting to the heart of a matter. Now here she was, digging into his psyche with a mere glance, telling him without words: maybe he needed to rethink God's direction.

A profound sense of loss descended over him. He knew, beyond a doubt, what God had just shown him. God made it plain He didn't care about income. He didn't care about prosperity. He cared about obedient hearts. And the parentless children being cared for.

God was calling someone like him who had the necessary know-how to get the word out: hundreds of teens were about to drop off a cliff unless God's people intervened.

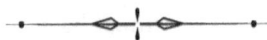

The reply from the Mercury reporter dropped into Myla's inbox less than an hour later.

> Dear BB:
> Thank you for contacting me. I appreciate your wanting to reach out to the Sausalito businessman to apologize, but I think it would be better if you contacted him yourself.
> Regards,
> Steve Davis

Still curled up in Bhree's corner, Myla shifted her cramped limbs and typed.

> Mr. Davis:
> I've been following your articles, and you might be interested to know what King-Boy's real name is. I know him personally—very well, I might add—and I know the general area where he lives. If you want to know, I'll tell you.

> Dear BB:
> You know King-Boy, huh? Tell me what the tattoo on his forearm is.
> Steve

Which one? The skull with snakes coming out of the eyeballs? Or the one that says MOM in calligraphy?
BB

OK, you do know him. Why do you want to identify him to me instead of to the police?
Steve

I don't trust the police. And you can get his name out to the public.
That would not be wise. He could sue the Mercury for libel.

Myla gritted her teeth as she typed.

Steve,
Then it also wouldn't be wise to tell you about a prominent citizen responsible for a lot of the opioid addictions in this county, would it?
BB

This sounds interesting. If you give me the person's name and the details of his/her involvement, I can put in a request to do an investigative piece. Assuming you are correct—Steve
I am correct. It was because of him I ended up a tent-dwelling, homeless addict.

CHAPTER

Forty-Two

Hell and destruction are before the LORD: how much more then the hearts of the children of men?

Proverbs 15:11 KJV

THE MARIN MERCURY

THAT HOMELESS LIFE
by Steve Davis

PART 6 OF A 6-PART SERIES

Well, friends, this is it. Yours truly is back at home and appreciating every precious moment of it. (So are my wife and daughter.) I will never take my creature comforts for granted again. I have a new appreciation for my Sleep Number mattress and even simple blessings like running water and indoor plumbing. Garbage service. Windows.

We've learned a lot these past few weeks, haven't we? We've learned who the homeless are, why they are living on the street, and why we are in an epidemic of drug addiction. And now, one glaring question remains: What now?

What can you and I, ordinary men and women, do about it?

We can keep writing to our state representatives and senators and ask them to make sure the state organizations which administer affordable housing services, addiction recovery services, and veterans' services are fully staffed and funded.

We can support the following non-profit agencies through volunteering and financial donations:

- Casas de Merced, a chain of five local drug and alcohol rehab centers for women, founded by Sisters of Mercy in the '70s.
- Transitional housing such as Our House and similar organizations that provide a place to live for addicts completing rehab.
- Eighteen Candles, a transitional service for foster kids aging out of the system.

Many, many more, both private and publicly funded, are just a Google search away.

But Steve, you ask, how do we make the addicts get treatment? You've shown how many homeless are simply one helping hand away from stability. We're totally on board with funding services for those people. But what about those who don't want help?

And what about those drug dealers?

I'll answer the second question first, then circle back to the first. It's simple supply and demand. As long as demand exists, the supply will never dry up. The reason the war on drugs failed is because it focused on the supply side of the drug trade. What if we were to reduce the demand for illicit drugs? How do we even go about accomplishing such a vague goal?

It has to start in the homes, schools, and communities. The state of California already has several school-based programs to help prevent substance abuse, but it varies in success and effectiveness from district to district and school to school. But there's hope. Remember the anti-smoking campaigns of the '70s and '80s? They were so effective the US smoking rates have declined since then by more than half. Today, what was once considered cool and hip has lost its allure. What made this dramatic shift in perception so successful?

The US Government, via the Department of Health, worked with private organizations such as the National Heart Association to launch a series of ads exposing the dangers of tobacco, and other groups worked with legislators to get smoking banned in public places by hammering on us about second-hand smoke. And we are all better off for it, aren't we?

How about we all work together to start a new war on drugs? But this time, let's co-opt the strategies of the Health Department and Heart Association and get the word out through advertising to vulnerable kids about how ruinous drugs are and how they can kill. I can just picture an anti-drug ad popping up on every smartphone game. Kids would have no escape, would they?

We need legislation to restrict doctors from prescribing hard-core painkillers like OxyContin to anyone under twenty-one. We can start locally and work our way out. The State Department of Education should enforce anti-drug education as a high priority in every school.

We can't afford to lose any more valuable persons to the streets, or worse. These are people who probably used to be a lot like you and me: dearly loved sons or daughters, hard-working employees, moms and dads to precious children.

In the meantime, we can learn from other communities such as Houston, which has dramatically reduced homelessness with a "housing first" philosophy and by coordinating multiple resources under one central umbrella.

Once the city gets them housed, then they can focus on rehabilitation. This is where your appeals to our state and local elected officials will pay off. It's going to require political will and courage to provide enough resources to rehabilitate hard-core addicts. Currently, rehab facilities in Marin County are woefully inadequate. Too many addicts combined with too few beds equals disaster. Yes, we need to throw more money at the problem, money to build and run many more treatment centers.

So, write those letters!

Comments

P.A. – Steve, with the "soft on crime" autocrats running this state, it's gonna be a long time before we see any political will. So far, all we got is political "won't!!!!!!"

V.W. – Bad idea. The war on drugs disproportionately affected minorities. It needs to be abandoned. Let's spend the money on education instead.

L.Z. – Our idiot governor has completely screwed up this state in every way possible. Border invasion, native Californians defecting to Arizona and Texas, while those of us who choose to stay get to see more graffiti and tent cities every day, not to mention broken-down RVs people actually live in. And the elites in Sacramento just sit on their thrones and let it happen. Our governor will go down as the worst in history and all of you who voted for him are to blame. Thank God I have a rifle, shot gun and a four wheel drive and this country boy will survive the coming second civil war!

F.M. – Our county leadership's track record on homelessness is dismal. Thank you, Steve, for lighting a fire under us and showing us practical ways we can help. I'm going online right now to donate to your worthy causes. Obviously, the private sector can do so much more than the public sector will!

D.R. – F.M., we need the public sector to step up. The non-profits can't do it all, nor do they have the clout needed. But the current approach of denial and head-burying is not working. Vote them all out and start over!!

A.M. – Speaking as a homeless person, all of you are wrong. A lot of us who live on the streets have jobs and need to be close to stores and our place of employment. You can't just move people into some 500-bed shelter and walk away feeling good about yourself. As soon as they have a chance, they're gonna sneak out and go back to their stomping grounds. I have utter contempt for those scumbag druggies, and I agree they need to go, but stop claiming we all need the same solution.

The Mercury – A.M., what is your story? How long have you been homeless? And what do you think we should do about the drug epidemic?

A.M. – A couple years or so. Can't afford rent, so I live in a double tent a block from the convenience store where I work. A lot of us live in double tents for security reasons. They're harder to break into, and they hold the heat better in winter. As far as the riffraff, arrest them and send them to jail where they can detox, like Rhode Island does. They are onto something, but God forbid California does anything so non-PC! I bet Rhode Island doesn't have drug addicts fighting on the street like we do. Once they're released after thirty days, they have to stay clean and stay in a state-administered treatment plan with Suboxone and accountability. What's good enough for little old Rhode Island is good enough for us.

Hey Steve, Jon texted. *I like your idea of a new war on drugs. What makes advertising effective is a line people remember, such as "Just Say No." How's this for a new slogan: "DON'T BE A STONER, BE A DRUG-FREE-ZONER."*

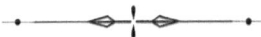

Loud knocking on Bhree's door sent Myla scrambling to her feet. Something about the loud force the visitor used sent a shiver of anxiety through her. It sounded like a cop knock. But what would a cop be doing here?

Bhree, sitting alone on the sofa after Miguel left to run an errand, raised her brows in a question. The TV blared a background accompaniment to the sudden tension in the room.

Myla rushed toward the bathroom. "If anyone's looking for me, I'm not here." She enclosed herself in the tiny room and sat on the toilet, one ear craning toward the door.

Male voices echoed outside, one of them Miguel's. "Where is she?"

Why would Miguel bang on his own door?

Bhree's voice: "She left."

He cursed. "I can't believe you'd invite a wanted criminal into our house."

"Wanted criminal?"

Another male voice, unfamiliar and deep. "She's wanted for burglary and vandalism."

Myla's heart leaped to her throat. Miguel had turned her in to the cops. What a creep. She needed any means of escape. The tiny window above the toilet invited a closer inspection.

But before she could even shift positions, someone jostled the locked doorknob, then more banging shook the bathroom door. "C'mon out, you criminal." Miguel's voice throbbed with anger.

She could tell from the first moment here he didn't like her. But to turn in a friend of his girlfriend's? How low could you go?

A key turned in the lock, and a uniformed policeman stepped inside. Ignoring her cowering form, he lifted her arm and pulled her upright.

"Myla Delaney?"

Sensing Bhree's confusion, she refused to answer. Why make it easy for them?

"You're under arrest for burglary and destruction of private property." Her head buzzed, and she tried to wrest her arm from his tight grip, but he wasn't having it. As he snapped on handcuffs, read her *Miranda* rights, and led her staggering from the apartment, her heart raced like a galloping horse, and her breath came in short, shallow bursts.

"If I tell you who did most of the damage," she gasped, "will it go easier for me?"

"Talk to your attorney."

"I will." If she could bust King-Boy, he'd be so sorry he'd abandoned her.

CHAPTER

Forty-Three

My son, despise not the chastening of the LORD; neither be weary
of his correction: For whom the LORD loveth he correcteth;
even as a father the son in whom he delighteth.

Proverbs 3:11-12 KJV

Tanner had gotten better at squelching the guilt pangs when he hung out with Ethan. As long as he made it back home before his dad did, his dad had no way to know what he was doing.

At least he wasn't doing drugs, despite Ethan's best efforts. "Dwyer always brings home the best weed from his work," Ethan told him. "You gotta try it. Mitch uses it for his back pain, and Mom even smokes it occasionally."

"No, I can't use pot and play baseball. We have to show them a clean drug test once a month, or we get kicked off the team."

Thank God for Junior League and his dad's encouraging him to play. He hadn't played much since his Little League days, and it felt good. Plus gave him an excuse to save face while declining Ethan's unwelcome offers of excellent weed. He couldn't tell his friend he would never use weed again.

Tanner's baseball excuse usually shut Ethan up, but not today. "Dwyer knows ways to obtain fake piss. You just keep it warm."

Tanner shrugged and returned to the pictures, enticing images which would get him grounded for all eternity if his dad knew. Ethan could be annoying and pushy sometimes, but he sure knew the best websites. Sites he couldn't access at home, thanks to his dictatorial dad.

When a heavy knock sounded at the door, they both jumped. Who could it be at four in the afternoon? Not his dad this time, he hoped. Mitch wasn't due home for another hour. Dwyer was at work, and who knew where the mom and sister were?

"Should I answer it?" Ethan spoke in low tones as if whoever stood on the other side of the door could hear him.

"Check the peephole."

They crept to the front door, and Ethan peeked through just as the doorbell rang. He jumped back, alarm widening his eyes. "Cops," he mouthed at Tanner.

Tanner recoiled. They must know about the illegal videos he and Ethan watched! Ethan's computer must have a tracking device! Maybe cool Mitch wasn't so cool and had installed something without Ethan's knowledge. He rushed back into Ethan's room and hid behind the door, visions of juvenile detention and his dad's shamed expression tormenting his mind.

Outside, Tanner heard Dwyer's car roar into the parking lot. Good. They'd let Dwyer deal with the cops. Dwyer didn't know what he and Ethan were doing in Ethan's room, so he couldn't rat them out.

Ethan darted into the room and over to the cracked-open window with a view of the parking lot. A warm breeze carried gently through the screen, along with the cop's firm voices greeting Dwyer. Ethan gestured Tanner over.

"What the …" A loud curse from Dwyer floated through the window screen. He must not have seen the cops standing in the recessed doorway until too late.

"We're looking for Dwyer Koningson. Are you him?"

"What for?" Tanner could hear Dwyer's hostility, visualize his fierce scowl. He wished he could see around the corner to the porch.

"Are you Dwyer Koningson?"

The other cop said, "He may have witnessed a crime we're investigating."

"According to the person who gave us Dwyer's name," said the deep-voiced cop, "you match his description. Why don't you come on down to the station with us so you can tell us what you saw?"

"I can't go anywhere right now. Supposed to be keeping an eye on my younger brother."

Tanner couldn't see Ethan's eye roll, but he felt it as sure as he stood here. Whew. He clutched the windowsill for support as relief the cops weren't after him left him weak in the knees.

"Not a problem," said the gentler officer. "We can interview you inside."

Shuffling sounds, followed by a slammed door, meant Dwyer had decided to cooperate instead of fighting it. Tanner couldn't wait to hear what crime Dwyer had witnessed. Had someone robbed the pot shop?

Or could it have to do with the hunch he'd been wrestling with for days?

He and Ethan crept toward the bedroom door and opened it another inch. The cop's voice carried as clearly as the sounds on Ethan's laptop. Ethan muted the volume.

"Please confirm your name is Dwyer Koningson."

"Yeah."

"Have you been in the vicinity of Waterfront Industrial Park on Bridgeway in the last six weeks?"

"Uh ... I don't remember. Not sure where it is."

"Do you know a young woman named Myla Delaney?"

Myla Delaney, the shop vandal? Connor's friend? Tanner sagged against the wall but not close enough to be seen.

When Dwyer replied, hard edges turned his voice into a sharp piece of metal. "Should I?"

"She claims you helped her break into a boat repair shop on …" The next words were muffled as though the speaker had turned away. "We have a warrant to search your home and car."

"For what?"

"An axe. She claims you took an axe to the boats and inflicted such severe damage they were completely ruined."

Tanner chewed his lips to stifle a curse. *Dwyer* was Axeman!

Dwyer swore again. "What bull."

The cop ignored his protest. "I understand your last name, Koningson, is German for king's son and you like people to call you King-Boy. You sell drugs in the homeless camps where they know you by that handle. We've found two people who can positively identify you. Tell us, King-Boy, where'd you get the drugs? How do you afford that slick red Charger you just drove up in?"

Dwyer's curses rang through the house as Tanner and Ethan crept into the hallway and peeked around the corner. Dwyer glowered as the cops snapped handcuffs on him. "Wasn't my idea!" he yelled as they tugged him toward the door. "It was my ex-stepdad who gave me the idea. You need to go talk to him and ask him how many addicts he's created with his legal Oxy prescriptions. Ask him about the kickbacks from the pharmaceutical companies. Ask him about the expensive vacations and his fancy house on the hill. Wonder how he can afford it all?"

"And who is your ex-stepdad?"

Between swear words, Dwyer managed to spit out, "He's a doctor down at Community Medical Center. Dr. Jenkins is his name. Dr. Tyler Jenkins."

CHAPTER

Forty-Four

Overhead, the Sausalito sky glittered with a million stars. A yellow pool from the porch light spilled over them as Meg rested her head on Jon's shoulder, letting the romance of the night soak into her heart. The light sweet scent of the wild roses settled over her and she released a pent-up sigh.

"Beautiful, my love," her husband's voice rumbled in her ear. "And so is the night sky."

"Oh, you." She reached up to stroke his whiskery chin.

"Penny for your thoughts."

"Just thinking about today. I think we had a pretty good first day at Eighteen Candles, don't you?"

"It was too chaotic. Way too disorganized. But I'm confident we'll get it under control."

"Can't really blame Chris and Isabel for letting things fall apart, though. I would've done the same in her shoes. I thought it was cute how she decorated the office with balloons to celebrate our first day. She's obviously excited."

He stroked her arms. "Unlike Kamala Yates at Phleet. I need to show you her email. She couldn't believe I turned down her offer, even upped the pay by 20 percent."

"I know you explained to her you'd been offered a life-changing opportunity with a non-profit, but she must've thought it was about money."

"I can't expect her to get it."

"Speaking of email, did you notice today how many emails and social media posts the ministry got?" Meg rubbed Jon's knee absently. "And we got at least two invitations to interview with local Christian radio stations. They're anxious to meet us."

"No way can we keep up with it all."

"True. Maybe we should consider hiring a Communications Coordinator."

"Needs to be a millennial. They're the social media experts."

"Hmm." Meg's mental wheels hummed. "Well, come to think of it, I believe we know someone in the right age range who needs a job."

"Who?"

"My son. He's totally an expert on all the social media sites. And he's got the personality for it."

"Yeah, he would be …"

"Dad?" They whirled, almost like a guilty couple caught in the act. But it was Tanner, silhouetted in the front door.

"What's up, Tanner?" Jon gestured to him to join them on the front steps.

"Want to hear something weird?"

"Absolutely. The weirder, the better."

Tanner sat on the top step and stretched his lanky legs in front of him. "So, um, I found out Dwyer got arrested today. You'll never guess what for."

"Knowing that family, it could be anything. Hit and run? Assault? Indecent exposure?"

"He was in on the break-in at your shop. He's the one who used the axe."

Meg felt the punch when Jon's arms tightened around her, and an almost-curse staggered out of his mouth. "Woah, seriously? I ought to … I ought to … You'd better not let me get anywhere near that kid, because I'm afraid I'd break most of the Ten Commandments."

"Why on earth would he do such a thing?" Meg said. "Did he even realize whose shop it was?"

"No clue," said Tanner. "He's just messed up. He's a drug dealer too. Sells Oxy and heroin at the homeless camps. And, um ..." He hung his head, staring at his twining thumbs. "You know that day on the boat when we saw someone at your shop?"

"Of course. What about it?"

"Um, uh, I thought I recognized Dwyer." Words flew from his mouth. "But I didn't think it could really be him. And then you started talking about Myla, and, um, I just thought ..."

"Thought maybe you were mistaken?"

"Yeah. I would've said something, I swear. But, uh, I didn't want to say it was him if it wasn't. He would've beat me up or something."

"Son, don't kick yourself. I get it. I really do."

Meg laid a hand on his arm. He reminded her of Eeyore on a bad day. "It's okay, Tanner. We understand. I wonder if he's the guy Steve Davis wrote about. Pharmer Boy."

"Farmer boy? No, he goes by King-Boy. The English translation of his last name. Bizarre, isn't it?"

Hard to believe the shop vandals had been right under their nose this whole time. Dwyer had to have known the shop was Jon's. He and Connor had been casual friends in high school, and Jon had never been less than kind to both Koningson boys. So why had Dwyer committed such a despicable crime?

CHAPTER

Forty-Five

*Be not deceived; God is not mocked: for whatsoever
a man soweth, that shall he also reap.*

Galatians 6:7

Dwyer, white-knuckling the jail's phone receiver, sneered at Jon from the other side of the partition. Jon decided to ignore Dwyer's hostility. "I just want to know why you did it, Dwyer."

Dwyer merely gave an indifferent shrug.

"Did you know the damage you did cost me my business?"

His gaze darting away, Dwyer drummed his fingers on the steel counter. Jon refrained from telling him how God had used his dirty deed to lead him and his wife closer to God's will. He didn't tell Dwyer what he truly wished to convey: if this had never happened, hundreds of foster kids might be left without support—baby birds thrust prematurely from unstable nests.

Jon persisted through Dwyer's silence. "Did I ever do something to offend you? If so, I hope you find it in yourself to forgive me."

Dwyer shook his head. Something flashed in his charcoal-dark eyes. Regret? Shame? But it vanished as quickly as it surfaced.

"You must have been very angry to cause that level of damage, and I'm sorry for whatever I did to enrage you."

"Wasn't about you," Dwyer croaked out.

"I'm glad. What was it about?"

"My stepdad is such a loser."

"In what way?"

"He makes us live in this little apartment, refuses to find a better-paying job than security guard." Bitterness laced his words. "When my mom was married to Dr. Jenkins, we lived in this huge, nice house on a hill. We could see the bay and everything. It ain't fair that Connor and Tanner get to live in a decent house with a view, and Ethan and I are crammed into this rinky-dink little box." Once the words escaped, they tumbled over each other in their haste. "The shop thing was Myla's idea, but it seemed like a way to level the playing field a little, if you know what I mean."

"I'm sorry life hasn't turned out the way you wanted, Dwyer."

"It ain't fair that I was making good money doing basically the same thing Dr. Jenkins does. It ain't fair that the law calls his drug dealing legal, but mine's illegal. What's up with that?"

Well, years of schooling and hard-won credentials, for one, but Jon kept it to himself. "I agree Dr. Jenkins should not have been so cavalier about prescribing opioids. From what I read in the paper, he regrets being so supportive of Big Pharma and accepting their kickbacks."

"Too late for regrets."

"Dwyer, can I pray with you?"

"Not here." Dwyer's facial muscles tensed, his gaze shifting side to side. "Do it on your own time, if ya don't mind."

"You bet I will." Jon tightened his grip on the phone. "Every day."

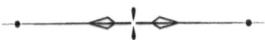

Meg blinked at Myla, horrified at her dark circles, the jumpsuit that appeared to have been slept in. Next to Meg, Candy tilted her pixie-haired head, her quick intake of breath betraying her identical shock.

Myla forced a sneer, but Meg could see the despair behind it. Compassion, not judgment, was in order today.

"Hi, BB. We came to say hello." And to ask why she'd vandalized Jon's shop, but God had clamped his fist on her heart and left a big-time check in her spirit. *Leave it in my hands*, she sensed Him saying.

Candy's eyes sparkled with unshed tears. "And to offer you a place to stay when you get out of here."

Myla cleared her throat, a sound like ashtrays and vapes. "Thanks." How did such a young throat produce a rasp like Bonnie Tyler? "Yeah, my lawyer says she can get me out of here on probation, 'cuz I'm, like, a first-time offender, so yeah, I'll need a place to stay." Her eyes darted everywhere but at their faces, finally settling on Candy's.

"I'll be happy to have you stay at my house, BB."

Another rasp of the throat. "It's gotta be better than this hellhole. My hearing is in two days, so I'll tell my attorney to contact you."

Why did you do it? Meg was dying to ask. At the very least, an apology would be appropriate. An awkward silence followed, during which Myla kept her head down, watching her fingers drum out a rhythm on the counter. She dared a scowl at the two security guards sitting just feet away, who watched their every move, and listened to their every word.

Myla finally let herself meet Meg's gaze. "Tell your husband I'm sorry." Her lips thinned as though in regret for saying too much, but Meg merely nodded.

"I will, BB. And as it turned out, God used it for good."

"How so?"

"Jon closed his business in order to run a non-profit called Eighteen Candles. Are you familiar with it?"

"Heard of it. Something to do with foster kids, right?"

"Yes. He's now working to make sure foster kids get the help they need when they turn eighteen."

Myla's mouth puckered as though she were holding back tears. A raspy sniff indicated said tears lurked just below the surface. "Wish I'd had that." A tear escaped, but at a lightning-bolt swipe of her fingers, it vanished, and her face smoothed over. "Hey, whatever happened to the dog?"

"What dog?"

"The dog I had when I passed out. It was JJ's." A glimpse of sorrow made its feeble way through a veil. "I was s'posed to be taking care of him."

"I see. The friend who was with me took him home with her. She's taking good care of him. I'm sure she'll be happy to return him to you when you're ready."

"Okay." She gave a hard swallow. "I've got to go. Best of luck to your husband."

She slammed down the receiver, swiveled, and darted back to the interior door.

Candy and Meg hurried back to the parking lot, Meg squinting against the sudden brightness of the sunlight. "Well. At least she apologized. I wasn't sure she would."

"But she still didn't tell you why she did it."

"I suspect it'll be a long time before she does." Meg fobbed her Mustang's door open. "God's going to have to work on her." She stared at her friend, striving to make her point. "And that's where you come in."

Candy climbed into the passenger seat. "God, help me. What have I gotten myself into?"

Meg started the engine. "You've gotten yourself a God assignment, my friend."

Forty-Six

The rod and reproof give wisdom: but a child left to himself bringeth his mother to shame.

Proverbs 29:15

THE MARIN MERCURY

A Sausalito man was arrested last Wednesday for prescription fraud and the illegal distribution of oxycodone pills. Dwyer Adam Koningson, 19, pleaded guilty to two counts of prescription drug fraud and five counts of illegal distribution. He has been sentenced to three years in California state prison.

A spokesman for Marin County sheriff's office, Kenneth Tucker, told the Mercury Koningson had been using the physician credentials of a relative to write up and print out bogus prescriptions for 90 to 120 pills at a time, using women friends as "runners" at various local pharmacies. He obtained prescription forms at the cannabis shop where he was employed.

Koningson, who went by the street name "King-Boy," was a frequent visitor at the local homeless encampments, where, he admitted, he had supplied oxycodone to the addicts.

Jon thrust the paper toward Meg. "Now I know how he did it."

"Who did what?" Meg pulled the paper through the pillar of steam from a fresh cup of Dark Roast and set it beside her on the island counter.

"Pharmer Boy, a.k.a. King-Boy, a.k.a. Dwyer." Jon took a sip of Dark Roast, puckering his lips. "You have to admit, he was pretty clever."

She scanned the article. "Indeed. He must have used Dr. Jenkins's registration number on the phony prescriptions."

"I'm pondering how this will impact Tanner's friendship with Ethan." Jon ran his hands over his already-mussed hair, a sure sign he'd been fretting for a while. "I'm afraid if I forbid him from hanging with Ethan, he'll just defy me. As he's already proven, he's capable of rebellion. But I don't know how much Dwyer's attitude rubbed off on Ethan. We need to hope and pray he won't follow in his brother's footsteps." Jon glanced at the kitchen door as if concerned Tanner could hear. Fortunately, Tanner had left for school twenty minutes before.

Meg rotated the kitchen stool back and forth, unsure how to answer Jon's concerns, then went to the coffee pot. The rich aroma drew her in for one more quick cup before she and Jon had to leave for the office. *For our Ministry,* she reminded herself.

Maybe she and Jon couldn't help every needy youngster. But they could certainly help the ones God put in their path.

And pray without ceasing.

Forty-Seven

Thank Heaven! The crisis—The danger is past, And the lingering illness Is over at last—And the fever called "Living" Is conquered at last.

~Edgar Allan Poe, FOR ANNIE

Five months later

The newborn baby's cry tore through the hospital corridor and jolted Meg from her seat. *At last!* Her new little granddaughter had arrived. She clutched Linzee's hand, but Linzee's own pregnant belly tilted her off-balance and into Ken's arms. "Careful, sweetie," he cooed, all protective dad-to-be.

Meg and Linzee hurried into room 125 and to Kassidy's side, who held her wet little daughter as Rich beamed like the proud daddy he was. Kassidy's parents, Jay and Faith Turner, rushed in seconds later. Meg squeezed in next to her son's newly bulky frame, his face aglow with joy and good clean health. With his new job at Eighteen Candles, his life was now complete.

Linzee bent down for a good view of the babe. "You go, girl." She fingered the baby's wet head, then patted her own protruding belly. "Your cousin's due to join you in just a few weeks."

Kassidy let loose a tired smile.

Linzee stroked the baby's velvet-soft cheek. "What are you going to name her?"

"Ember. Ember Simone St. John."

Little Ember's mouth formed a tiny O, but her loud wails contradicted her miniature size. Kassidy snuggled her against her chest, and the wails stopped as she and Kassidy gazed in awe at each other. Dark blue eyes latched onto pale gray ones, the glue of age-old mother-baby bonding.

"Yo, Mommy." A nurse reached for the baby. "Time for a quick bath for babe, then I'll bring her right back for her first feeding." She whisked the whimpering baby away as Meg's heart throbbed at the blessings God had showered on her and Jon. Healthy kids, healthy grandkids. A beep interrupted her musings, and she left the others to bask as she found a chair and read the text from Candy.

Myla went into labor!! Heading to the hospital as we speak! Look for us to arrive soon!!

Meg breathed a quick prayer for the health and strength of Myla's baby, then replied.

My new granddaughter just arrived! See you in the maternity ward soon!

She grinned at the irony of the two babies being born on the same day, in the same hospital. God works in mysterious ways, as they say.

She sent photos and updates to Connor and Tanner, then texted Jon to find out when he was arriving. After she'd texted him of the impending birth this morning, he'd rescheduled his meeting with a state senator in Sacramento, then reversed direction at Vacaville to return home and provide support to her and Rich and Kassidy.

Here was the opportunity she'd been hoping for. A chance for Jon to confront Myla and extend grace.

But would he?

The pastor had spoken on grace just last Sunday. "Just as we want God to extend grace to us for our wrongs, so should we extend grace to others when they disappoint us."

Her phone beeped.

I'm here.

She told him where she was and returned to Kassidy's bedside. The new father held and cooed at his daughter. "Little Ember, born in September. Mwah mwah." Ember regarded him in wonder as he planted kisses on her tiny cheeks. Conversational buzz floated around her as everyone offered opinions on the new babe.

Jon strolled in. "Where is she?"

Rich held her out. "Here you go, Grandpa."

When the hubbub subsided, Meg pulled him aside as he cradled Ember. "Hey, I found out something interesting just now." She relayed the news of Myla's baby, concluding, "Sounds like God is orchestrating an opportunity for you."

"What kind of opportunity?"

"To extend grace. Like Pastor talked about last Sunday."

She heard the you're-right resignation in his sigh. "Okay, fine. But is she going to even want to see us when she's in labor?"

"If we time it right."

Ten minutes later, she got the text. "Honey, time to go see Myla."

They found Candy and Myla at admissions. Myla's hair, still short, had returned to its natural brunette shade, and Meg almost didn't recognize this new, non-gaunt BB. Candy saw Meg before Myla did and waved them over.

Myla's face contorted, and a nurse escorted her to a seat to wait for someone to take her back. Meg nudged Jon. "Here's your chance."

As they approached, an invisible curtain draped Myla's features. Meg smiled to show the young woman they meant no harm.

Jon stopped in front of her and spoke first. "Myla, it's good to see you again."

She merely stared at him—her face etched with discomfort. From labor or awkwardness, or both, Meg couldn't tell.

"My wife and I want you to know we're praying for you, and if you need anything at all, please let us know." He took a business card out of his pocket and handed it to her. "I mean it. Call us with whatever you need."

"Thank you." She lifted her gaze, latching onto Jon's. "Sorry for everything." She took the card, a tiny smile hovering, her eyes more alive than Meg had ever seen them. "Hey, could you ask Connor if I can call him sometime?"

An amused smile from Jon. "I'll pass it along. Take care, now."

A nurse with a wheelchair arrived and took Myla away, followed by Candy, who waved at Meg as she disappeared behind the double doors.

Meg and Jon, hand in hand, returned to Kassidy's room. "Way to emulate Jesus, Hon." She squeezed his hand. "Let's go see our granddaughter now."

As they approached the room, a flash of red rushed at them. "Connor!"

"Dad! Meg." He pulled off his red knit cap and stuffed it into his jacket pocket. "Hey, just came to see my new niece. Ember, right?"

Meg took him by the arm and stopped outside the room. "Ember Simone. And you'll never guess who else is having a baby right here, right now."

"Uh, Myla?"

"How'd you guess?"

"Stab in the dark. You told me she was pregnant." Two pink spots snuck into his cheeks. "She's here now? Having her baby?"

"She is. And ... she wants you to call her."

Connor, stifling a grin, lifted his phone. Meg stopped him with a chuckle.

"Not now, silly. She's in labor! Just send her a text and ask her to call you when she's ready."

He turned away and lifted his phone, but not in time to hide his toothy grin.

A warm beam poured hope onto the already heaping pile in her soul, and she entered the room filled with cooing and laughter.

Connor would be so good for Myla.

Lord, let it be.

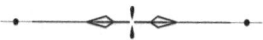

In room 130, Myla snuggled her plump newborn baby boy and kissed his pink, healthy cheeks over and over, finger-caressing his impossibly soft head, drowning in the depth of his indigo eyes studying her.

Grinning at her birthing coach, Candy, she led baby Liam to the milk source he sought. At the first painful jolt, she expelled a gasp, but after a moment, the incredible high of her infant nursing overpowered her, mocking Oxy's fake euphoria. She sighed, relishing the sight of his tiny bobbing head, letting the joy sweep her away like an ocean wave. Yeah, this was the real thing, the thing Oxy tried to accomplish but couldn't.

Candy reached a hand to the babe, and Myla grasped it, grateful for Candy's support. "Look at this beautiful, healthy little boy," she croaked out, exhausted yet exhilarated. "Guess you were right to make me take those supplements and take better care of myself."

"Hey, it's what I wish someone had done for me," Candy whispered back, both of them somehow infected with the reverence of the moment. "I'm just paying it forward."

"I can't tell you enough how grateful I am you gave me a home when I most needed it, and you gave me a chance instead of judging me."

"It's the least I could do."

"I had nothing. Totally nothing."

"Yet today you have so many blessings to count," Candy reminded her.

True. Sister Louise, for one. She wished Lou could be here right now. In fact, she needed to send the good sister a photo of Liam along with a thank you note. She knew exactly what she needed to say.

A composition formed in her head. "Thank you, Sister Louise, for your kind attention to my trauma. And for launching my healing journey. I was hurting so badly after I lost Lula. And now, look what God has done. He's given me another baby, Liam, who's healthy as a horse. God is a redeeming God, just like you said.

"Thank you for encouraging me to seek legal action against Tyler. You'll be glad to know he settled out of court, and the settlement money will tide me and my child over for many years.

"And thank you for pointing me to Jesus: my Higher Power, my Savior, my Redeemer.

"Love, Myla."

The End

Dear Reader

Recently, I watched a heart-rending, appalling YouTube documentary on homelessness in a certain US west coast city. The hosts filmed block after block of shanty-like structures, ragged tents, trash, and graffiti, and compared it to Haiti. They blamed several factors: rampant drug use, lack of law enforcement, indifference by city policy makers, high rents.

In the scenic west coast city where I live, I have seen in person the tragic after-effects of the opioid crisis, chronic narcotic addiction, and out-of-control housing costs. In my city, it might not appear as bad as what I saw in the video, but it sure appears to be headed that way. With all the blue tents blocking sidewalks (the tents and tarps are given out by the county, I've learned), the piles of trash, the ugly graffiti and broken-down RVs, my city has become unrecognizable. Crime has soared, and people are concerned.

But why? Why didn't we see this scene ten, fifteen years ago? What has happened to our nation?

If you live in a major US metropolitan area, you have likely been affected by the homeless crisis which has exploded in the past ten or so years, especially in the states of California, Florida, and New York. In this story, I aimed to humanize the problem by setting part of the story in a homeless camp. In my own experience with a homeless outreach ministry, the houseless folks I chatted with one-on-one proved to be real people like you and me who had either gotten caught up in addiction, or some other misfortune had victimized them. But so many others have been hardened from years of substance abuse. These are some of the ones either doing the victimizing, or they are capitalizing off the addicts.

I also found, as illustrated in this story, numerous reasons why people end up on the street. But too many times public policies try to solve the problem with a singular focus instead of getting to the root cause or emphasizing prevention. Perhaps it takes too much individual investment and time? Yet I am thankful for the many non-profit organizations and ministries who do take time to tailor individual solutions. In my opinion, however, there just aren't enough of them. As my fictional county official said, the problem is exploding faster than we can solve it.

This is not merely a liberal or conservative problem. Blaming the other side won't solve anything, yet too often I see pointing fingers on social media. Just like the fictional commenters, it's easy to blame the other side, or the prevailing political powers-that-be. In my opinion, we can only solve the problem through practical, sacrificial means, and by being willing to invest time and resources into individual lives.

If you're interested in learning more about the opioid crisis which has swept the nation in the last twenty years, I recommend the book *Dopesick* by Beth Macy. She highlights several families who've endured the tragic death of a loved one from drug addiction, and some of the grass-roots efforts to hold the drug companies and medical professionals accountable.

Another fascinating book is *Dreamland: The True Tale of America's Opiate Epidemic* by Sam Quinones. Each chapter highlights a different city and tells a different tale of tragedy or triumph. A well-written, informative book, you will learn a lot about the underground drug trade in the US you may have been unaware of.

As the books in my Hot Topic Fiction series demonstrate, it's clear there are no pat or easy answers to complex social problems. But individual believers can do a lot. Together, we can be the hands and feet of Jesus, and I hope I made those options clear in this story, the conclusion to my Golden State Trilogy.

If you enjoyed this story, please leave feedback on social media or any review site. Thanks!

Blessings–
DVC

Acknowledgments

This novel wouldn't have been possible without assistance from some wonderful folks offering their expertise.

Thanks to Steve Mathisen, Odd Sock Proofreading and Copyediting. I thank you for your contribution in making this a stronger manuscript. To Dineen Miller, my talented cover designer. You're the best! To Leanne S, beta reader, for your helpful feedback. Thank you for your honesty in pointing out what worked, and what didn't. To my nurse friend Cheryl H., who told me everything I needed to know about drug detox and rehabilitation, and patiently answered all my questions. I appreciate it more than I can express. I named my kind fictional nurse who tended to Myla during her hospital stay after you!

Thank you all for your roles in this exciting project.

About the author

Dawn V. Cahill, an indie author from the land of microbrews and coffee snobs, published her first book, When Lyric Met Limerick, in 2015. She published her first full-length novel, Sapphire Secrets, in January of 2016. "The characters in my stories face situations which would have been unthinkable even 20 years ago. We live in a vastly different world than our parents did, and that's the world I write about."

Seeing an unfilled niche in the Christian market for edgier fiction, Ms. Cahill came up with the concept of Hot Topic Fiction (HTF) at an intensive four-day writers conference. HTF isn't afraid to explore the question, how does God want us Christians to live out our faith in this not-so-brave new world? Without insulting the reader by offering pat or easy answers—because there aren't any—HTF tells stories of ordinary Christians following hard after Christ in a world of terror and violence, of upside-down morality, of hostility to Judeo-Christian values.

She has written six novels, several newspaper articles, and more limericks than she can count. Email her at dawn@dawnvcahill.com, or find her on Facebook, Twitter, and her website. She is a member of Oregon Christian Writers (OCW) and American Christian Fiction Writers (ACFW).

www.ingramcontent.com/pod-product-compliance
Lightning Source LLC
Chambersburg PA
CBHW030255200626
46816CB00002BA/647